D

This book is dedicated to those that have love troubles

That like reading about love troubles

Or can identify with Bridget Jones

Chapter 1

"If you walk out of that door, we are done – we are over." I hesitated. My mind wavered. Whilst I loved Rob, I had had enough of his controlling behaviour. I wanted to leave, but was I really ready to leave behind my entire life?

At the age of 29, my life plan wasn't really working. I'd hoped to be settled down by now. I'd wanted to be thinking about starting a family. At this rate I'd be a geriatric Mum, if I managed to become a Mum at all.

But enough was enough. I needed a fresh start. After two years of living with Rob, I'd finally decided that the constant rollercoaster of a relationship with him was too much.

I took a deep breath, put my hand out to the door, turned around and said "Goodbye Rob. I've had enough. I will be in touch about collecting my things in a few days." And I left.

I rocked up to my Mum's house 45 minutes later. However old I get, I always seem to end up back at my Mum's house. At least there I know I will get a sympathetic ear, a big hug – and of course some good food.

"Of course you can stay" said Mum. "You know there is always a place for you here."

"Thanks Mum, I really appreciate it" I replied.

"So what was the final straw?" Mum asked. For months I had been keeping Mum updated on the trials and tribulations of living with Rob.

"I told him that I was going out for Molly's birthday tonight. He didn't want me to go." For some reason Rob tried to drive wedges between myself and my friends. He seemed to want me all to himself and often stopped me from seeing my friends or going out. I always invited him, but he just didn't want to be sociable with other people. Rob was quite a bit older than me – he was 39, so maybe that was part of the reason he didn't want to hang out with my friends.

"And you aren't going to go back to him again this time?" enquired Mum.

"Definitely not – I'm done this time" I stated.

It was true that I had had a couple of temporary splits with Rob in the past. And poor Mum had had to listen to my troubles. And then watched as I ended up going back to him. But not this time. It was final this time. It was time to start again. Otherwise I could see myself in a continuous loop, always wanting to be happy but never quite managing it.

I picked up my phone and called Molly. I brought her up to speed on what had happened and made plans to meet up with her and some other friends for a night out for her birthday. Molly was pleased as she knew I was more likely to stay out and have fun without the thought of having to go home to Rob at the end of the night. She was never that keen on Rob really – they just tolerated each other.

"3, 2, 1, go" shrieked Molly. The 4 of us all banged our shot glasses on the table and downed them in one. Our faces as the vile mixture burnt down our throats was amusing and we all burst out laughing at each other. The music was loud, the lights were flashing, the atmosphere was rocking and we were all having a great time. It was a long time since I'd really let my hair down and had fun. It was great to feel a real part of the social circle again. In the last couple of years I'd only been out a handful of times, hadn't drunk very much and had felt rather outside of my friendship group. Well, that was all over now. I felt totally confident that I'd done the right thing in leaving Rob. I was back in with my besties, and looking forward to starting afresh. It actually felt like a weight had been lifted from my shoulders.

"Let's hit the dancefloor" shouted Molly. We all grabbed each other's hands and waded onto the dancefloor. The music was awesome and we spent half an hour or so dancing to some excellent dance tracks from the 90s. At last, hot, sweaty and rather thirsty, we headed back to the bar for drinks, and then made our way outside for some fresh air. I was drinking cider (my favourite) and the other girls were drinking a mix of WKD and vodka/cokes. Everyone was having a good time but we needed a little breather.

Whilst we cooled down in the night air, I brought the girls up to speed with my splitting from Rob. They were all totally supportive. Whilst he was a good looking chap, he had never made much (if any) effort with any of my friends, so they all agreed with my decision to move on. We started to shiver so decided to head back inside and have another round of shots. This always seems like a good idea at the time, but no doubt I would suffer the next morning. I was staying at Molly's flat tonight so that I didn't disturb Mum by coming in very late. I knew she would stay awake waiting for me if she was expecting me home, so it's better to stay elsewhere after a night out.

An hour later we realised that it was 2am and started to think about heading home.

"Chips, chips, chips" yelled the girls so we headed towards the chip shop. We were weaving about the pavement, a little worse for wear. But hungry – oh so hungry. We stormed into the chip shop and ordered. We all wanted chips with cheese. It's amazing how brilliant they taste after a long night out.

As we waited for our chips to be served to us, the door opened and two guys walked in. They looked in their early 30s, and both of them were really good looking. One was tall, blonde and had a dazzling smile whilst the other was dark and had piercing brown eyes. Molly & I looked at each other and raised our eyebrows. We instantly knew that I would be attracted to the blonde and Molly would be attracted to the dark haired lad.

"Evening ladies" said the blonde chap. "How are you? Have you had a nice evening?"

"Oh yes thanks" replied Molly. "We've had a top night celebrating my birthday".

"How old are you today then? 25?" he asked.

Molly laughed, that would make her happy.

"I'm 29 today" replied Molly. She was just a bit younger than me.

"Well I'm James, and this is Harry" replied the blonde.

"Good to meet you James. My name is Molly, this is my best friend Lily, and these are Evie & Georgia".

Our chips arrived, so we headed outside and started eating them.

"Let's wait for those lads" said Molly. "They were nice".

Evie & Georgia decided to head off – they were going to share a taxi to the village where they lived a few miles away. We said our goodbyes and agreed to meet up again soon.

The two boys then arrived and we started to chat to them whilst eating our chips. They told us that they both

4

worked for an engineering firm in the nearby town. They were best mates and shared a flat together. They were keen on sports – both watching & playing them. James (the blonde) was a runner and Harry played rugby. That made me quite excited as I have recently started running. I told James that I had done the local parkrun a couple of times. What a small world. He has also run the same parkrun but only on a few occasions. We decided to swap numbers, as did Molly & Harry. It was then time to head for home. James & Harry were heading in the same direction as us, so we all 4 shared a taxi. That was a bonus as it was half the cost. In fact, the boys insisted on paying as they were going past us in any case, so we jumped out first after a free ride.

We bundled into Molly's flat, laughing and giggling. We both tripped up the stairs trying to race in the quickest, so probably made far too much noise. I'm sure her neighbours won't be happy. Hopefully we didn't wake them up. Molly heads to her bedroom and I head to the sofa and I'm pretty sure that we both crashed out instantly. After a night of dancing, drinking & chips, we had no chance of staying up chatting.

Chapter 2

Oh my god. My head is banging. There is a tiny man with a hammer inside my head. The rhythmic blows with the hammer are driving me insane. My mouth is dry – so dry I can't even swallow. I think I might actually die. I sit up. The hammer blows have got even more painful. I need some painkillers – and I need them now.

I get up, wobbling across the carpet and head into the kitchen. I open up the mess draw where the painkillers live – thank goodness. The familiar packet of aspirin are lying there waiting for me. I take two and chug them down with some water. I head to the fridge. I need Coca Cola. I don't know what it is about coke, but it is amazing when you have a hangover. I'm fully aware that coke is full of absolute garbage, but it certainly helps cure a hangover. I pour myself a glass and then pour another for Molly. I take her two tablets and head to her room. She is still asleep. I leave the glass beside her bed, with the aspirin ready. She will be pleased to see that when she wakes up.

I head back to the sofa and collapse. I close my eyes and start to drift off. If I can get back to sleep the painkillers should work and I will feel like a new woman when I wake up. I hope.

An hour later I wake again. My head feels so much better. The hammer has gone. I've still got a dry mouth, but I feel miraculously better than I did. I can hear Molly wandering around the kitchen so I head out to see her in my pyjamas.

"Morning Hun" I say to Molly. She turns and smiles at me holding her head.

"I just woke up. Thank you for leaving the drink and the painkillers by my bed. I'm really grateful".

"No problem at all. Do you feel as rough as I did earlier?" I enquire.

"Not too bad considering" replied Molly. "I've felt worse – mind you, I've felt much better too. It was worth it though. We had a great night. I really enjoyed it. Thanks very much".

"An absolute pleasure honey. I really enjoyed it too. It's been ages since I let my hair down".

"Do you remember meeting James & Harry at the chip shop?" asked Molly. I had actually forgotten about that. I smiled.

"They were nice – good looking too. Where did they live? I can't remember?" I said.

"They lived just a couple of miles past here remember? We shared a taxi home with them". So we did. It was all coming back to me now. I remembered putting James's number in my phone. I headed back into the lounge to pick up my phone. As I did so, I noticed that I had a text from James.

How's the head?

I wanted to reply straight away, but I do know that that is not the cool thing to do. Whilst I don't like playing games, I didn't think it best to reply straight away. So I made a mental note to reply later.

"Shall we head out for breakfast Molly?" I asked.

"That's a good idea" she said. "I could murder a full English".

"Me too. I'm starving. Which is silly really seeing as we ate chips & cheese last night" I replied. I'm always starving hungry when I've got a hangover.

We headed downstairs and into the street. The sun was shining, the birds were singing. There was a lovely café just a few doors away that was a regular haunt of ours. We headed there and swung open the door.

"Morning girls" said Patrick, the owner. "Take a seat and I'll be over shortly".

We picked our normal table in the corner. Whilst I hadn't been out with them many times recently, I did occasionally meet up for breakfast. Rob used to be out rowing on a Sunday morning, so I was often at a loose end. To be honest, Sunday mornings had really become my social life. Sad really. I made a mental note to stay away from controlling men in the future.

Patrick headed over to take our order.

"Please can I have a full English, no black pudding though, crispy bacon" I asked.

"And to drink?" Patrick asked.

"Earl grey tea please – oh, and can I have a pint of diet coke as well please?" I said.

Patrick laughed. "Heavy night?" he enquired.

"Just a bit" I laughed.

Molly ordered the same, minus the diet coke. She had a latte instead. She loved drinking coffee of various types. Not something that I liked at all.

We spent the next hour enjoying our food, laughing and talking over the events of last night. We'd both had a fabulous time and decided we must do it again soon. Next Friday was payday, so we arranged to head out again Saturday night.

Later that morning I headed back to Mum's house. Mum said that she would come with me to pick up my stuff from Rob's flat. It would probably be a few car loads. I'm not big on clothes, but I do love to read, so my book collection alone would take a trip or two. I texted Rob and he said he'd be out all afternoon, so I was welcome to pick up my stuff.

When we arrived, my stuff was already packed in boxes. It made me a little sad, but at least we both seem to agree the relationship is over. I left him a note thanking him for packing up my stuff. I didn't really expect to see him often, he didn't really go out much and he worked about an hour away in a different town. It felt bizarre that I'd gone from living with someone, to just not seeing them at all anymore, in 24 hours. Very strange indeed.

When we got back to Mum's I decided to text James back. That would cheer me up after a rather miserable afternoon.

I felt pretty rough first thing – but a full English with Molly solved the problem.

A couple of hours later James texted back.

Glad to hear it. I went out for a 5km run. I felt pretty rough at the start but by the end I felt back to normal.

That got me thinking, and I decided a run would be a good idea. I put on my running gear and headed out towards the local park. It was a mile to get there, I did a couple of circuits, and then took a different route home. A total of about 4.5 miles. I felt good, the sun was still shining. I saw a fox running into the woods, and I met a few people walking their dogs. It was very uplifting and I went home feeling positive and happy. I always feel better after a run.

James had texted again. That was quick.

Want to meet up for a drink one evening this week?

He seemed a bit keen. Which is good, but made me a little bit wary. When you first meet someone new it is difficult. You want them to know that you like them, but equally you need to keep them guessing a little to start with. I liked James. He seemed nice. He was good looking. A fresh beginning was maybe just want I needed. But, I'd only just split up with Rob. Was it too soon? I decided to call Molly and see what she thought.

"Go for it" said Molly. "It will give you something to look forward to. You've had a crappy few days and you deserve a bit of fun. Just don't go jumping in with both feet." Molly then told me that she had had a text exchange with Harry as well.

"Maybe we could double date?" I suggested.

"That's a good idea" Molly agreed.

So I texted James back and suggested that we meet up Thursday evening with Harry & Molly too. Everyone seemed to think that was a good plan. I was pleased to have Thursday to look forward to. I wasn't really looking forward to work tomorrow. Whilst I enjoy my job, Monday's are always a little wearing. I think it's just getting back into work mode after a weekend can be a little hard sometimes.

Chapter 3

Monday morning rolled around. It didn't start well as I forgot to set my alarm so I was 20 minutes late for work. John (my boss) gave me a look and told me that I would have to make the time up. He was obviously in a bad mood today. This annoyed me as I rarely took a lunch break – it was usually spent scoffing a sandwich whilst working at my desk.

I was an assistant editor on a magazine. John is the editor and I work alongside him. What this actually means is that he does the editing of all the interesting articles, and I get the boring ones. The writers are a nice bunch though. I like working with them, and we have some fun. The magazine is called Athletics UK. It covers all types of athletics events. The large, international & national competitions make up the first half of the magazine, and in the second half we run a number of articles on related topics – warmups, health tips, nutrition, workouts and so on. I tend to do the editing for most of them. I enjoy it, it's fun and I get to learn quite a lot too.

I spend a long day at work, and end up working until gone 6pm. So I more than made up for the slightly late arrival this morning. Even John was in a good mood by the end of the day as it had been very productive. The magazine is issued weekly, and goes to print on a Wednesday, so it's good to be in front by the end of Monday. Tuesdays are always spent completing the results of the weekends competitions which are sent to us throughout Monday. If they miss the cut-off they might not make it into the magazine – or maybe delayed until the following week.

It's an interesting place to work – it's fast, it's busy, and you can never get bored. Other than Mondays, I do enjoy my job. It's just getting back into work-mode that can be a little difficult at the start of the week.

On the plus side, Mum lives much closer to work, so I can walk now rather than having to drive. This will mean I can save some money on petrol and do my bit for the environment.

As I'm walking home that evening, a text comes through from James.

How was your day?

He's quite keen. Texting already. I wasn't expecting to hear from him until Wednesday or Thursday. I decide not to reply until later. I know the rules of the game at least.

As I enter the house Mum walks into the kitchen to put the kettle on.

"Fancy a cuppa, love?" she asked.

"Yes please. I'm parched" I reply.

We have a catch up about our days. Mum works part time in a newsagents just down the road. She's not been to work today. That sounds blissful. I'd like a part-time job, but it's just not possible to earn enough money only working part-time. I am going to have to save up now to get enough for a deposit for a new flat. Whilst Mum is very kind, I really don't want to have to live at home for very long. We get on well, but I can see the relationship could be rather tested if I'm home for too long.

I bring Mum up to speed on James. She seems pleased that I've met a nice chap and she approves of our plans for Thursday. Molly has been single for quite some time, so she is extra pleased that she has a date to look forward to. I express my concerns that it's a bit early for me to date really, but Mum agrees with Molly. She advised me to just take it a day at a time, and even though I have just split up with Rob, she tells me to look forward and focus on a fresh start. I think she feels that it will help me move on and prevent me from going back to Rob.

After a nice evening, chilling out with Mum, I head off to bed. We have decided to start watching a box set. We looked at our options and decided on '24' starring Kiefer Sutherland. I've seen it before but not for about a decade – and Mum hasn't seen it at all. There are plenty of series to watch, so at least it will mean that we won't argue about what to watch on the TV in the evenings.

Chapter 4

It's date night. I'm excited. It's been a long time since I last went on a date. Molly and I have been texting back and forward all day discussing what to wear. I'm not really into fashion but Molly is. She has quite interesting taste – she loves wearing dresses and bright colours. I'm more of a jeans and top kind of girl.

We have arranged to meet the boys at 7.30pm at a local bar. It's a cocktail bar which is fun, if rather expensive. I hope we won't stay for too long in there as I can't really afford to drink cocktails all night. On the plus side – it's walking distance from Mum's house so I don't have to pay for a taxi. I will go back to Mum's tonight as I'm working tomorrow so we won't be out for a late one.

I arrive at 7.20pm and Molly is already there. James is also there and the two of them are chatting. They haven't got drinks yet. Harry strolls in a few minutes later – he's come straight from work as was on a later shift than James. It's good to see them both, and I feel excited to see them and to have a double date. I actually have that butterflies feeling. I've not felt that for a long time. James gives me a hug and kisses my cheek. He's very polite.

"So Lily, how's your week been?" smiles James.

"Not bad, thanks. It's been busy but that's a good thing I guess. How about you?" I reply.

"It's been a good week thanks, other than our garden shed got broken into and both Harry & I had our bikes stolen. That's a bit gutting."

"Oh no, that's terrible. Have you been in touch with the police?" I asked.

14

"Yes" replied James. "But they aren't interested. We just got given a crime number and that was it. They didn't even bother coming out. I guess they have better things to do".

James & Harry headed up to the bar to buy us a cocktail each. I hope we go somewhere else before it's my round. Cocktails, lovely as they are, cost a fortune. We did have a good giggle at the names of the various cocktails though as most of them are rather rude.

The boys heading off to the bar gave Molly and I chance to catch up.

"I'm really excited to see Harry" said Molly with a thumbs up.

"I'm pleased to be here too, although I'm not really sure I'm ready for anything just yet. It's only been a few days since I split up from Rob" I replied.

"Have you heard from him yet?" asked Molly

"No, I haven't" I replied. "I thought I might, but nothing yet." I had been musing on this for the last couple of days. I wonder if Rob has actually missed me at all?

By this time the boys returned with a cocktail for each of us. I had a sex on the beach, and Molly had a strawberry daiquiri.

"So how long have you been single?" asked James.

"I only split up with my boyfriend on Saturday" I answered. James looked a bit surprised about this.

"Oh, I'm sorry to hear that. Had you been together long?" he asked.

I explained that I had been living with Rob for 2 years. But that he had become rather controlling and tried to stop me seeing my friends. The relationship itself had gradually deteriorated into a toxic mess.

"I can't stand people who are possessive" said James. "There is just no need for it".

"I completely agree" I replied. "It became very tiresome over many months. Finally, when he said that I shouldn't go out for Molly's birthday that was the last straw. We had a big row and I left".

"Have you seen him since?" asked James.

"Nope" I replied. "I think we both realised that the end of our relationship had come. He went as far as boxing up all my belongings and left them ready for me to pick up on Sunday afternoon. I've not heard from him since. So I've moved back in with my Mum for the moment".

"Wow" said James. "I had no idea. You had quite a traumatic weekend then. Perhaps us meeting was fate. Perhaps it was meant to be".

I was quite taken aback by this comment. It seemed a little presumptuous to me. I wasn't sure I was ready for a new relationship, excited as I had been to meet up with James tonight.

"I'm not sure I'm really ready for a serious relationship" I said. "I feel like the sensible thing would be to have a break, get my life sorted again, find somewhere else to live. But, I have to admit I was very happy to meet you on Saturday night, and I was excited to meet up with you again tonight".

"Well that's fair enough" said James.

"So how about you?" I asked. "How long have you been single?". I'd had enough of talking about my situation and wanted to find out more about James.

"I've not had a proper relationship for over 2 years" answered James. "My last long term girlfriend moved away to live in the US with her dad. So it kind of finished by accident. I've dated a couple of times since then, but not found anyone that I like enough to move beyond that".

"So what's the worst date that you've ever had?" I asked. I felt like I wanted to lighten the atmosphere a little bit.

James pondered for a minute or two. Then he said.

"I've got it. This date was hardly believable. I had been chatting to this girl that I met on a dating site. I'm not really keen on dating sites to be honest, but I hadn't met anyone for a while, so thought I'd give it a go. I actually only went on it for a week and I'd had enough by then. Anyway, this girl seemed really nice. She was cute. A sporty girl. She seemed fun and had done lots of exciting things in her life……"

"But – I take it that the date didn't go to plan?" I asked.

"Ha – you can say that again. She texted me to say that she was going to have a barbecue and did I want to join her and her friends. Bear in mind that this was to be our first date. I'd not met her before. I said yes, I'd love to come. She told me where she lived. So I rocked up with a bottle of wine and some flowers for her. I thought that was a nice gesture" James said.

"I would say so. I'd be quite happy if someone did that for me" I said.

"Well, unfortunately it went pear shaped from there" explained James. "As soon as I arrived it became evident that the young lady in question was drunk. Not just a little bit drunk but very drunk. There were 4 or 5 others at the BBQ but Tara (that was her name) was worried about a chap called Stephen who was a friend of hers who hadn't turned up. He had been drinking with Tara earlier that day and had nipped home to get more alcohol but hadn't come back. She was worried that he might have got in his car and driven it, as that had happened once before when he had been drinking. She decided to leave the BBQ and go and look for him. She didn't seem to give a damn that I was there, she hardly spoke to me and then she left to go and look for Stephen....".

"Did you speak to her before she left?" I asked.

"Yes, I told her that I didn't think anyone that drove after drinking was worth worrying about. She seemed very offended by that comment and said that a friends place is to look out for her friends. I guess you could say it was our first disagreement, and then she left".

"So what did you do?" I asked.

"I hung around for about 10 minutes and then gave up. I certainly hadn't been very impressed by her behaviour or by how she spoke to me, so I left. I sent her a text later that day saying thanks for the non-date but she didn't even bother replying. So I think that qualifies as my worst ever date. How about you? What's your worst ever date?"

I think carefully. I have had a few shockers really.

I reply to James "Well, I think my worst date was when I met up with a friend of a friend for a blind date. I hadn't met him before but our mutual friend was convinced that we would suit each other. I've heard that one before" I laughed. "We met up in a pub, had a single drink together, and he started talking about his hobby – which was train spotting. Well, I couldn't get away fast enough. When I said I was leaving because I had an early start the next day, he asked me if I wanted to go train spotting with him at the

18

weekend. He seemed most taken aback that I wasn't interested." I laughed again.

James joined in and we both continued to laugh. We then started to chat a little more with Harry & Molly who were also getting to know each other a little. We heard their stories of their worst dates too. Harry had been to dinner with a girl and then her parents turned up to meet him. That put a stop to any desire to meet up again. And Molly's worst date was with a man she had met on a dating site who had turned up looking at least 20 years older than his profile picture. She'd been blunt and told him to do one straight away. No point even having a date with a man old enough to be your dad.

The evening continued and we chatted & laughed. When it was my round, I shared it with Molly so that it didn't cost too much. Both the boys seemed to have more money than us, so it worked for everyone. We soon realised we had better go home as it was technically a school night (well not really school of course, but we all had work tomorrow). The four of us planned to meet up again on Saturday night in town. Although James and I both said that we might make it to parkrun on Saturday morning first. I had been planning on going the last couple of weeks, so meeting James there would be another reason to get myself out of bed on Saturday morning.

James & Harry walked me home together as they were walking past Mums house anyway. Molly got a taxi home – we waited until she had left before we started walking. I crept in the house quietly but Mum was awake anyway – so I updated her on the evening. She was pleased to hear that I'd had a good time and that Molly had also enjoyed it. It had been slightly awkward saying goodbye with Harry stood next to James, but he didn't try to kiss me, which is probably a good thing. I'm not sure I'm quite ready for that – although I also kind of hoped he would. Maybe next time.

Chapter 5

Friday passed quickly in another whirr of work and an evening watching boxsets with Mum. It would be good for my 'saving money' drive. Mum kindly treated us to a Chinese takeaway though, so that was a nice gesture. About 8pm, just as I was settling down with Kiefer Sutherland, I received a text from James.

Evening Lily, how's it going? Are you still up for parkrun in the morning?

Yes. I'm staying in chilling out tonight, so I will definitely be there bright, early and bushy-tailed. See you there if you can make it.

I'm looking forward to it

Saturday morning rolled around, and I climbed out of bed at 7.30am for a quick breakfast of white toast. By 8.45am I was stood at the parkrun gathering point chatting to a couple of people that I knew slightly. I saw James jog into the park and he came straight over.

"Good morning, how are you?" he asked.

"I'm great thanks. Looking forward to a nice run. I've only done parkrun a couple of times so far" I replied.

"I've run it around 10 times" James replied. "What kind of pace do you run at?" he asked.

"I'm don't trouble the leaders" I said. "Very much the middle of the pack. My PB so far is 32 minutes."

"Well my PB is around 22 minutes" James replied, "But I will gladly run with you if you would like my company?"

"That would be lovely" I replied. "As long as I don't hold you up too much".

"Of course not" said James, "It's always more fun to run with friends".

We were then all asked to quieten down as it was time for parkrun briefing. The man in charge told us about the parkrun rules and the course and then it was time for the off.

"5, 4, 3, 2, 1 parkrun" he said after checking that the timekeepers were ready.

We set off. A little too fast for me, but we soon settled down to a pace more within my comfort zone. James and I chatted lightly on the way around. We talked about our jobs, our living arrangements, a couple of friends that we both knew. James was nice and easy to talk to. The course was a 3-lap course – a mixture of grass and woodland tracks. It was very picturesque and I felt very happy. Even the weather was kind today – a very light wind, a nice bit of sun but not too hot.

When we started the 3rd lap, James looked at his running watch.

"You are running brilliantly Lily" he stated. "You will be well on for a PB if you keep this up".

"I'm feeling pretty good today" I replied. "And that would make me very happy if I achieved a PB".

"Well, let's try then" said James. "Do you think you could go just a tiny shade faster?"

"I can try" I said. I started pushing a little harder. James carried on chatting to me, but I was struggling to answer back now as I was running out of my comfort zone. James reassured me to not try and talk back and to focus on running and breathing instead.

A few minutes later we were at the last corner. I'm not really a sprinter, but I tried my best and I did manage to increase my speed quite a bit. I pretty much collapsed over the line and just about managed to take my finish token before having a lie-down on the floor once I'd moved out of the way of the other runners.

"Let's catch our breath before getting scanned" said James. I wasn't yet able to talk back as I was still struggling to breathe.

A few minutes later we made our way over to the barcode scanners. We presented our personal parkrun barcodes and then our finish tokens.

"What time do you think we finished in James?" I asked.

"You were fantastic" he replied. "We were well under 31 minutes, so a definite PB for you".

I was delighted to hear that. I was hoping eventually to get under 30 minutes so it looked like I was one step closer to achieving it.

"What are you doing today?" I asked.

"I'm playing tennis with Harry this afternoon, and I have a few jobs around the house too. And then of course we are looking forward to meeting up with you and Molly later tonight".

"Fabulous" I replied. "I'm looking forward to tonight as well. I need to sort out my belongings at Mum's house and pop out to a couple of shops. I really should start calling it home. Anyway, I will see you later".

James left and I walked back to Mums. I felt very happy. Almost like I should be skipping along like a young girl. Things were looking up. And I felt extremely proud when a text came through from parkrun later that morning to inform me that I had a new PB of 30 minutes and 34 seconds. That is a massive improvement…. I was buzzing.

Chapter 6

I spent longer than normal getting ready for our date night tonight. But that was only because Molly came over and we drank some wine whilst getting ready. Molly, as always, took forever to get ready. She came over with four different outfits to try on. She finally settled a red summery-dress which looked a combination of sexy & sophisticated. I settled for skinny jeans and a crop top.

We met up with James & Harry in the cocktail bar once again. This time we were only planning to stay for a single round which the boys shared between them. I had a Moscow Mule and Molly stuck with her Strawberry Daiquiri. The boys had a Mojito each.

I proudly told Molly & Harry about my parkrun adventure this morning. They were both impressed and pleased for me. Harry had been to parkrun once before but really didn't like it. He is more of a team sports player. Molly refuses to run entirely. She is not keen on getting sweaty & dirty.

We started talking about Sunday and going on a trip somewhere. We fancied going to a rollercoaster park but it was quite expensive and not really what I needed to be spending my money on at the moment. I explained to Harry about having to save up for a flat deposit.

"I've got it" exclaimed James.

"What?" I asked excitedly.

"The perfect day out for the four of us" he said. "How about we hire a punt for the day, take a picnic, a few beers, and have a nice lazy day on the river and head upstream to Ceasar country park. It's always quiet there and there are loads of places we can spread out and enjoy a picnic".

"What a brilliant idea" exclaimed Molly. "I love it. As long as I don't end up in the water that is."

"Me too" I said at the same time as Harry.

We chatted excitedly about tomorrow's adventure - the food and drinks that we would each contribute, the time & place to meet and so on.

We had soon finished our cocktails, so we headed down the road to a busy pub that had a dance floor. We didn't really fancy going to a nightclub again this week, but Molly and I did fancy a dance. The boys didn't seem quite so keen but said they would join in.

When we got to the pub Molly and I went to the bar. This time we bought pints for the boys, and half pints for the girls plus a vodka each and a can of redbull to share. Whilst we didn't want a heavy night we knew that it would give us all some energy for dancing.

After finishing the drinks and downing the vodka, we proceeded to dance. James & Harry were both quite good dancers so we had a really good time with them. About 6 or 7 tracks in a slow, soppy track came on and we decided it was time to leave. We were planning an early start the next day and none of us wanted a heavy night. We arranged to share a taxi back with the boys again as we did last week.

This time when we said goodbye, James gave me a kiss on the lips and a hug. It was really nice. He smelt of a really nice aftershave, and felt warm and comfortable. It wasn't a full on snog, but a nice teaser for future days. Molly & Harry were having a full on kiss, but I didn't really feel ready for that quite yet. James seemed to understand and said that he didn't mind waiting as long as was required.

Once the boys had left in the taxi, Molly & I had a hot drink in the lounge, chatting excitedly. She is really into Harry and he seems like a really nice lad. Equally, I really like James too – other than being a little wary as I don't want to jump into a new relationship too quickly. However, we are both really excited about punting and a picnic tomorrow. Neither of us have been punting before, so that will be a new experience. And of course, we both like to eat, relax & drink so we are looking forward to the picnic too. We decided we would take a rounders bat & ball so that we had the option of having a game of rounders if we fancied it.

We bid each other good night, and I settled down on the sofa while Molly went to her bedroom. I fell asleep straight away and had a wonderful night's sleep.

Chapter 7

I woke up at 7.30am feeling rather better than this time last week. I'm glad that I didn't have a killer hangover again, plus, I was really excited about our trip today. It was ages since I'd had a day out with friends especially including a guy that I was keen on.

I wandered into the kitchen to find Molly already up and about. The kettle was on and she was eating some cereal. I poured myself a bowl as well and we chatted excitedly about our trip. We nipped out to the nearby shops to get some food for the picnic. We had decided that we would provide the bulk of the food and the boys would bring some drinks – both soft and alcohol. Whilst it's nice to have a few beers, none of us wanted to have too much on a Sunday, as we were all back at work tomorrow.

Molly and I bought a range of food. Sausage rolls, scotch eggs, some sandwich making things, some ham, some cheese, and a small punnet of strawberries. We headed back to Molly's flat and made a stack of sandwiches. We added some fruit to the stack of food and dug a few paper plates and plastic glasses out of the cupboard. We grabbed a picnic blanket and a small hamper that Molly handily had tucked away in a cupboard somewhere.

By 8.45am we were ready to leave. I was carrying a rucksack with the picnic blanket and the plates/glasses and some bottles of water. Molly had the hamper with the food. We met up with James & Harry at the boathouse where the punts were hired from. They were already waiting for us, and had big grins on their faces. James gave me a hug and a quick kiss on the lips, whilst Molly & Harry had more of a smooch.

I was really pleased to see James, and I could tell that he was pleased to see me too. His eyes crinkled at me when he smiled and he had a little dimple in his cheek. It was really cute and I felt butterflies in my tummy again. James grabbed my hand and we started walking towards the boats.

"How are you?" asked James. "You look fantastic".

I'd not really known what to wear so had settled on some jean shorts, and a white linen blouse. I'd worn converse trainers as we'd probably play some games later on.

"You look pretty hot yourself" I replied. And he really did. He wore some navy shorts and an open neck shirt. He was tanned with really sexy forearms. I like the forearms on a man – they need to be brown and strong. James certainly ticked those boxes.

James & Harry had already sorted out which punt we were going to be using. I could see that they had already put a bag into the punt. They steadied the boat whilst myself and Molly climbed aboard. The punt rocked a bit as we got in, but we felt fairly safe. The boys passed us the hamper and then jumped in themselves.

"Anyone had a go at this before?" asked Harry.

"No" we all replied.

"Me neither" said Harry. "This could be amusing."

Harry stood at the back of the boat with a long pole. He used the pole on the side of the river to push us away from the edge. He then used the pole on the bottom of the river bed to push us upstream. Luckily it was very still today, so easy enough to navigate upstream.

"Where are we going?" I asked.

"We are heading upstream" replied James. "Towards Ceaser country park. It's not too far and it's lovely once we get there. We can tie up the punt and picnic in the park. And then it won't be too hard coming back as it's with the current.

"That sounds great" I said. "Can I have a go later?"

"Of course you can" agreed Harry. "We can all have a go".

We'd already gone around the first corner and the boathouse was now out of sight. It was quiet, the sun was shining. I could hear lots of birds in the trees, and the steady sound of the water. It was blissful. I felt very happy and relaxed, and pleased to be on a day out with friends. The river itself was quiet with just the occasional punt or small boat visible.

"Are you going to have a go at punting?" asked Molly.

"Definitely," I replied. "I'm really keen to have a go. How about you?"

"Maybe" said Molly. "I'm not that bothered."

"Well, I like trying new things, and I've never had a go at punting before, so I'm definitely up for it".

James smiled at me. He really did have a cute smile – he smiled with his eyes as well as his mouth. It made me want to smile back at him.

It was a beautiful day. It was late spring-time which is my favourite time of year. The spring season seems full of hope and promises of the summer to come. Everything starts growing, the land is green and beautiful. Across the river I could see fields of sheep and lambs. I could hear them calling to each other. It was warm but not too hot and there was a decent breeze. We didn't have to worry about sunscreen, but equally were warm enough in shorts and t-shirts.

The next 30 minutes was spent easily chatting & laughing as Harry and James took turns to punt us upstream. The four of us really did get on well and it was really nice to get to know the boys a little more. Molly & I had been friends for a very long time, so we knew each other really well. But it's always exciting to get to know new friends and potentially more. Whilst I hadn't really felt ready for a new relationship a week ago, the more I got to know James, the more keen on him I was. I suddenly realised that I hadn't even thought about Rob for the whole day. That's quite amazing really, considering just over a week ago I was still living with him.

I jumped up making the boat sway from side-to-side.

"Sorry," I said. "I didn't mean to make the boat rock. Can I have a go please?"

"Of course," replied James who was punting at the time. "Come over here and we can swap places".

"On my way," I grinned at him.

I clambered over Molly and the picnic hamper and made my way to the end of the punt. I reached out for the long pole from James. He stood behind me and put his arms around me to guide my arms into the correct place on the pole. He explained how to push the pole into the river bed and then push off it to guide the punt upstream.

"You try now" he said. And moved away from me to sit down.

The first couple of thrusts went well. I pushed down on the pole and then allowed the punt to glide

30

upstream. The next time I pushed down on the pole I did a larger thrust to get the punt moving a little quicker. This time however, as I attempted to lift the pole it seemed to get stuck. The punt didn't stop though and I could feel myself being tipped towards the back of the boat.

"Don't let go of the pole" shouted James.

I held onto the pole as hard as I could whilst attempting to keep my feet in the boat. This was not quite going to plan. I still couldn't release the pole.

The next thing I knew there was no boat underneath my feet. Uh oh, I knew what was coming next. With no boat underneath me, I slid into the water fully clothed. My god, it was cold. I totally submerged with a scream and this time I let go of the pole. Luckily I was a good swimmer so there was no real concern, except there were reeds around my legs. This must be what the pole had got stuck in.

"Do you need me to jump in and help you?" worried James.

I glanced back at the boat. James looked worried but Molly and Harry were just laughing their heads off. There was no real danger, the river was pretty still, I could almost touch the bottom although it was rather reedy so nicer to tread water.

"I'm fine" I answered. "I just need to rescue the pole".

The pole by this point was floating on the surface of the water a few feet away. I swam over to it and then dragged it back towards the punt. James was looking rather relieved and reached out to take the pole off of me. He then passed it to Harry so that he could help me back into the boat. It wasn't the most lady-like of scrambles back into the boat. It was however effective. I belly flopped back into the punt with a bit of helpful tugging from James on my waistband. I was cold & drenched, but no harm done. Molly was still laughing at me. It was pretty infectious and now that I was back on board I laughed too and the boys joined in.

"I'm freezing" I said. "I'm definitely ready for a picnic now."

"No worries" said Harry, "the stopping point is only about 50 metres away. I will get us there so we can get moored up. "Molly – pass Lily a towel – there's one in my rucksack".

Molly passed me a towel and I used it to mop up the excess of water and give my hair a quick dry. By the time Harry had tied up the punt to the mooring point, I was feeling a little better. We all hopped out of the punt and made our way up the incline into the sunshine.

Molly pulled out a couple of picnic blankets and we all collapsed. I lay down in the sunshine hoping that I would dry off quicker. Luckily the warm temperatures and the breeze would dry me off in no time. Maybe that should be the end of my punting career.

Molly then grabbed the hamper and arranged the food on the picnic blanket. The boys also had a few bits and pieces to add to the mix so we had quite a feast to enjoy. The boys had brought some lager and cider so we each grabbed a can and sat back to relax and enjoy the picnic.

Whilst eating and drinking we carried on chatting. James and Harry told us about a recent trip that they had made to Snowdonia for a camping and hiking weekend. It sounded a lot of fun to me although Molly wasn't quite so keen. Camping is not her thing at all. She would have been a terrible girl guide.

Once I had dried off, the afternoon was a roaring success. We chatted, we ate, we had a couple of cans each. We had a game of rounders and we lay in the sun relaxing and talking. I hadn't had as good a day as this for a long time.

Eventually, 4pm came around and we had to head back as the punt had to be back at the boathouse by 5pm. We were all sorry to leave but had had such a great day. The trip back was rather less eventful and much quicker. We debated heading to a pub for a couple of hours but we all had work tomorrow and things to prepare for that. So we bid each other farewell and headed towards home. I was sure it wouldn't be long before we met up again.

Once I got home Mum was out which was a bit of a relief. I wanted to chill out rather than detail my day to her. I knew she would want to know everything and I was shattered and had some prep to do before work tomorrow.

That night I slept well. Really well. Obviously punting, swimming, sunbathing & rounders was good for tiring me out.

Chapter 8

On Monday night James texted me.

Would you like to go to dinner with me on Wednesday night? Just the two of us?

That sounds great. Yes please

Great – I will meet you at the Hammer & Horses at 7.30pm?

See you there

I was quite excited about meeting up with James. It would be the first time that we had had a date alone. It's quite different spending a whole evening alone with someone else, rather than double dating with friends. I also really like the Hammer & Horses. While it is a pub, it's not a drinkers pub. It's a really nice restaurant pub. The food is Italian and absolutely gorgeous. It is my favourite place to eat.

Wednesday night came around. James and I had exchanged a few texts over the last couple of days but we had both been pretty busy. I decided to actually wear a summer dress for our date tonight. I'm not really a dress-up person, but I thought I'd make an effort. Plus I did have this one, really nice, sky blue summer dress. It had little shoulder straps and was about knee length. It wasn't particularly sexy – more cute than sexy really. I borrowed some sandals from Molly to wear with it. It was a nice warm evening so I just had a light cardigan over the top.

I walked to the Hammer & Horses from Mum's house. It was only a 15 minute walk and was a lovely evening for a stroll. When I got to the pub it was just gone 7.30pm and James was already seated at a table for two. He looked really tasty and was sipping a gin & tonic. Definitely an ideal summer drink. I approached the table and James looked up.

"Wow," he exclaimed. "You look sensational."

Well that put a smile on my face. I was glad I had made the effort to dress up just a little at that comment. Rob had never really complimented me much, so it was a nice change. I also felt yet more butterflies in my stomach. I really did like James and was excited about our date.

"Thank you, you are very kind. And you look pretty good yourself" I replied with a smile. I couldn't help but smile at James. He just had such a nice, warm and welcoming smile.

James jumped up.

"What can I get you to drink?" he asked.

"I'll have a glass of sauvignon blanc please" I replied. I wasn't a big wine drinker but I do enjoy it with a meal.

"That's a good idea" said James. "I'll get a bottle and we can share it. I quite fancy wine as well".

James headed off to the bar and placed our order. He was back a few seconds later as the waitress was going to bring the wine over.

We started chatting about our week. Neither of us had been up to very much other than working. I asked James what he had planned for this coming weekend.

"I'm not sure yet," James said. "I'm probably going to go and do parkrun again – if you fancy joining me? And then maybe we could do something later in the day as well?"

"That sounds good" I replied. "As long as it's cheap. What do you fancy doing?"

"I was thinking we could go to the open air swimming pool for the afternoon? We could chill out, do some sunbathing, have a picnic and do some swimming. What do you think?"

"That sounds like a good idea. I've not been swimming for ages. Are you a good swimmer?" I asked.

"Yes, pretty good" responded James. "I fancy having a go at a triathlon this year. I like swimming, I'm fairly decent on a bike and as you know I enjoy my running. So I'm definitely tempted by the challenge of a triathlon".

"That sounds fun" I said. "I can come and cheer you on".

"Perfect" laughed James. "That's a plan".

The evening progressed. There were no awkward silences and we had lots to talk about. We ate a gorgeous meal. I had a tricolore starter which is avocado, mozzarella and tomato. It's absolutely delicious. And then I had a plain steak with new potatoes and vegetables. It was scrumptious.

James had garlic mushrooms to start, and then a vegetarian pizza. By the end we both were full, a little tipsy from the wine, and feeling very happy.

"Shall we take our drinks outside and sit in the garden?" asked James.

"That sounds like a good idea" I replied.

The garden was small and secluded – and empty. We sat next to each other and James put his arm around me. I relaxed into him. He felt warm and smelt amazing. His aftershave is really nice. It felt really good to sit with him.

36

I looked up and could see that James was looking down at me. I looked into his eyes and then my gaze moved down to his lips. I really wanted him to kiss me. His gaze did the same and I really hoped that he was thinking the same thing. I lifted my lips up towards him and he moved downwards towards me. Our lips came together. I felt a spark of excitement. I hadn't kissed anyone new for nearly three years. It's such an intense moment.

We kissed gently. I felt his tongue move into my mouth. He was a fantastic kisser. Gentle but curious. Sometimes you meet someone that you could just kiss forever. James was definitely one of those. He made my heart beat quicker. I didn't want to let him go. I was glad we were the only people in the garden as I'm not really into PDAs (public displays of affection).

We broke apart and smiled at each other. It seemed he enjoyed the kiss as much as I did. We spent the next half hour finishing our drinks and kissing. A lot. There was a lot more kissing than there was drinking. It was great. I felt really happy. However, it was getting late now. The bartender had been outside to get our glasses so it was really time to go home. James walked me back home and we had a fantastic kiss before he left. I even saw a twitch of the curtain so I knew Mum had looked out. But I really wasn't bothered. I was sure she'd be happy for me. I would have to introduce them soon, but now was not the time. It was too late for a start and we both have work tomorrow.

After a final farewell kiss I went inside the house. My face was a little sore from James's stubble. I wasn't used to kissing this much. I had a chat to Mum and told her about my evening. She was looking forward to meeting James and seemed happy for me. She had never been that keen on Rob so she was pleased I had moved on.

That night I fell into a deep, dreamless sleep. I woke up the next morning smiling as soon as I remember the kisses. I really did feel fantastic – and incredibly excited every time I thought about James. In fact, I needed to tell myself to tone it down a bit. After all, I had only just met James really. It was too soon to be getting too attached.

Chapter 9

I ate breakfast with a smile on my face. I thought back to the date with James and felt a contentment travel through me. I picked up my phone and there were two text messages. The first was from James and said:

Morning gorgeous. Thanks for a great night. I really enjoyed it.

I replied.

Good morning to you too. I had a great time too. Let's do it again soon.

James responded immediately.

For sure, will text you later. Have a good day.

I then looked at the other text that I had received and started to frown. It was from Rob.

I miss you.

That was all it said. I looked at the time it was sent – 12:14am. He had had a late night then. I guess Rob had been drinking. I debated whether to respond and then decided not to. What was the point? I didn't want to restart things with him, and he was probably regretting sending the message anyway. Best to just ignore it. It was time to get up and get ready for work in any case.

The remainder of the week flew by. I had a few text exchanges with James and had totally forgotten about Rob texting me. When I got home from work on Friday there was a bouquet of flowers that had been delivered. Mum had already received the delivery and she handed the card to me.

"Do you want me to put them in a vase love?" she asked.

"Are they for me?" I replied. I was very surprised. Who would be sending me flowers? I doubted it would be

James. Whilst we liked each other, sending flowers was for birthdays and anniversaries. Not just when you'd had a couple of dates. I picked up the card.

I miss you. Please can we chat soon? Love Rob.

I was very taken aback. I showed it to Mum. She also looked really concerned.

"What are you going to do now love?" she asked.

"Well, I don't really know. I have no interest in going back to Rob. I'm quite happy moving on and I'm enjoying getting to know James. I certainly don't miss the rollercoaster of the relationship that I had with Rob. It was hard work – stressful. I really don't need that".

"I think you are right love. Sometimes the best way is to move onwards and upwards. Don't look back".

I did feel a little bad though. Two years is a long time, and whilst Rob had seemed to initially agree with me that it was best to split up, he now appeared to be changing his mind. I chatted to Mum and we decided it would be best to send a text to Rob. I didn't want to see him and couldn't see what that would achieve. I decided to speak to Molly to get her advice. I picked up my mobile and dialled her number. After some initial pleasantries we got down to business. I explained that I had received the text a few nights back and now a bouquet of flowers. They looked pretty expensive too.

"Oh no," exclaimed Molly. "So, what's the plan? What are you going to do? Are you going to talk to him?"

I explained that I had no intention of meeting Rob face-to-face. I, perhaps surprisingly, hadn't really missed Rob, and was happy to be moving on. I told Molly that I was just going to send him a text, but that I wasn't really sure what to write. We chatted back and forth for a while and decided that I should send the following:

Thanks for the flowers – which were very beautiful. However, they are unnecessary. I'm not interested in discussing our relationship any further. It's best in the past. I'm moving on and I hope that you are too.

It was quite harsh, but I didn't really see the point in giving him false hope. I had no intention in meeting up with him again.

I didn't get a response, so I hoped that that would be the end of it. I hadn't told James what had happened. It didn't really seem necessary. To me it was just the final chapter. In my head, that relationship was done and dusted.

Tonight Molly and I had arranged to meet up with James & Harry again. This time we decided that we were going to go to the cinema. The local cinema had new seats where they were in pairs so you could snuggle up together. They were really comfy and it would be nice to cuddle with our men. They even reclined so you could put your feet up, lie back and enjoy the movie.

We had a slightly heated discussion about what to see. The boys wanted to see the latest action movie by Guy Ritchie, and us girls fancied a romcom. We decided on a compromise. We would watch the action movie this time, and then the next cinema visit we girls would get to choose.

James arranged to pick me up. Mum was really excited because she wanted to meet him. She'd only seen him outside for a minute or two. I sighed. It seemed a bit early to me, but in view of the current living arrangements, I guess that it made sense for them to meet.

"Let's keep it low-key though please Mum," I suggested. "I will invite him in and we can have a quick drink with you before we head out."

"Perfect" responded Mum. "I'll pop to the shop and get us a nice bottle of sauvignon blanc".

"Good idea" I replied. That was my favourite wine and I knew that James would be happy with a glass or two.

An hour later James had arrived. I let him in and he gave me a kiss. He also had some flowers with him. That was kind – and unexpected. I said thank you but he laughed and said,

"Sorry, they are not for you. They are for your Mum. As I'm taking you out and leaving her on her own, I thought she might appreciate some flowers".

"That's really kind" I replied. I really did think that was a nice touch. We headed into the kitchen and I introduced James to Mum. James handed over the flowers to Mum and explained why he'd bought them for her.

She looked very happy as she said thank you. She actually went a little red in the cheeks. Mum then reached for a vase from the cupboard and filled it with water before arranging the flowers and placing them on the windowsill. On the other windowsill was the other bouquet of flowers. I was pleased when James made no comment on those as it might have been slightly awkward had he known that Rob had sent the other bouquet. Mum handed both James and I a glass of wine, and she picked up hers.

"So James, are you from here originally?" Mum asked.

"No, I'm from Brockenhurst in the New Forest originally. My parents still live there. It's a lovely place to grow up and I do like returning to visit". James said.

"Is that the place where there are wild ponies and donkeys that roam the streets?" asked Mum.

"That's right" responded James. "There are all sorts of wild animals. There are the ponies & donkeys, deer, foxes, badgers, snakes and even wild boar. It's an amazing place to visit. When it rains you often get donkeys and miniature ponies sheltering in the shop doorways. It's quite an experience".

"It sounds blissful" I commented. "I've never been to the New Forest, and I'd love to visit one day".

"Well next time I go home you will have to come with me" replied James.

"That sounds great. I will look forward to it" I said excitedly.

"Actually," said Mum. "You have been to the New Forest, but you were only about 7 or 8 so I would imagine that you don't remember it much. Do you remember going crabbing once upon a time?"

Actually, on reflection, I did remember the crabbing. Although I don't really remember the setting for it. I remember it being really good fun and I was gutted when we had to leave.

"We went crabbing with some friends in Lymington, which is just a few miles from Brockenhurst. It's a truly beautiful part of the country to grow up in. You were very lucky James," said Mum.

We chatted for a little while longer. Mum really seemed to warm to James which was a relief as she had never really liked Rob very much. After I finished my wine I suggested that we head off. We said goodbye to Mum and walked into town. It took 25 minutes or so to get to the cinema but it was a lovely evening for a stroll.

Once we arrived we met up with Molly & Harry. We loaded up with diet cokes, popcorn and some chocolate and made our way into the cinema. We really enjoyed the movie, snuggling up with each other and munching our way slowly through the giant popcorn buckets that we were sharing. It was a really relaxing, pleasant evening.

After the movie finished we followed the train of people outside. We decided to head to a popular bar just down the road for a couple of drinks before heading home. It was fairly busy in town tonight and a good atmosphere. As we entered the bar, James & Harry said they would get us some drinks. Lily & I were stood a few feet back avoiding the crowds.

Suddenly there seemed to be a commotion. I didn't really see what happened but there were shrieks of alarm and a lot of pushing and shoving. The next minute there was a major scuffle involving four or five different guys with James in the middle. It looked like James got hit in the face and fell to the floor. The security guard for the bar came running over and quickly broke up the scuffle. As he led away the perpetrator I thought it looked like Rob, but I couldn't really see due to the lack of light and the number of people milling around.

I ran over to James who had a nosebleed and a cut lip. I asked him what happened.

"I was just queueing to get us drinks at the bar and this guy suddenly barged into me, seemingly deliberately" he said. "I turned around to tell him to be careful and he suddenly punched me in the face. I don't even know who he was or why he did it".

"It looked like my ex, Rob" I said. "I wonder if it was him?"

James asked if I had a photo of him on my phone – which of course I did have quite a few. James poured over

44

the photos and said that it could have been him, but he really wasn't sure. We went to talk to the security guard but he didn't know much more. He said the troublemaker had scarpered as soon as he'd got near the door so he didn't get a chance to question him.

It took us a few minutes to sort James out. His nose was bleeding for quite some time. We were all rather subdued after what happened and decided to call it a night. James walked me back to Mum's house but we decided against kissing again as his face looked sore. It was still early so we went inside and put a cold compress on his mouth and nose to try and reduce the swelling.

We also told Mum what had happened. I would have been quite surprised if it had been Rob who had behaved in such a way, but it had looked like him. We discussed going to the police (something the security guard had suggested) but the bar's CCTV wasn't working and there was really no major harm done. James decided it wasn't worth pursuing and that he would just chalk it up to experience.

Half an hour later James headed home and I went off to bed. What a shame the evening had turned out as it did.

Chapter 10

It seemed only a short time later that I was suddenly woken up by a loud bang. I was very confused and squinted at the clock which said 02:02am. I sat up in bed and listened – I was sure I could hear a tinkling of glass. Suddenly there was an immense cracking noise and I leapt out of bed. The window had caved in and something rolled towards me. I screamed out loud from pure fear.

I reached for the light switch and the room flooded with light. A large rock was sat on the floor of my bedroom and one of the window panes was broken. There was bits of glass everywhere. I could hear Mum shouting for me and I called back that I was ok. She hurried from her room to mine and stopped in astonishment in the doorway, looking at the carnage. What on earth had happened?

I wrapped my dressing gown around me and headed downstairs. I switched on the outside light but there wasn't anything to see. I couldn't see anybody outside and I certainly wasn't brave enough to go outside looking. It seemed obvious that someone must have thrown a stone through my window. But who? And why?

Mum & I went into the kitchen and picked up the dustpan & brush, some newspapers and a couple of bin bags. We swept up the glass and the rock, wrapped it in newspapers and dumped it all inside the bags – one inside the other to ensure it was strong enough. When we had finished we took it downstairs and left it by the back door. We then put the kettle on and made some tea.

We settled on the sofa in the kitchen to discuss what had happened. We had already decided there was no point involving the police. They just wouldn't be interested in a rock through the window. It was most likely just local kids who were bored and causing trouble. We did discuss whether it could possibly be Rob. I wouldn't have dreamed he would do something like that but after the punch that James took from someone who looked quite like him, it was a possibility. He was quite possessive and controlling so maybe this was a form of jealous behaviour? I still struggled to really see him doing this though. This is a very juvenile behaviour, and he is definitely not that way inclined. Plus, he didn't exactly fight for our relationship at the time, so why would he be quite so bothered now?

After an hour or so chatting, I couldn't stop yawning. I headed up to my room to get my duvet and then laid down on the sofa. I wasn't going to sleep in my room which was now rather cold and not properly secure. We taped some cardboard over the missing window pane, but there wasn't much more we could do in the middle of the night. We would have to get the window mended in the morning by a glazier.

I spent the next few hours tossing & turning on the sofa. I couldn't sleep properly. Every time I dropped off I heard a funny noise which woke me up again. I think I was still shocked from the rock being thrown through the window. The sofa was also nothing like as comfy as the one at Molly's house. I finally dragged myself up around 6.30am to make some tea. After a nice cuppa I felt marginally better and made some bacon sandwiches for Mum & I. At least the house smelt good and once I started eating I realised that I was actually quite hungry. Feeling satiated, I nursed a second cup of tea and made some plans with Mum.

Mum kindly encouraged me to head to parkrun rather than wait for the glazier with her. She was happy to stay in and get the window sorted. I called James and he popped over for a cuppa before we headed off to parkrun together. He was shocked about the breaking of the window, and his face looked really sore where he had been punched last night. He suggested we contact the police, but Mum & I weren't so sure. Eventually we decided we'd call them and see if they wanted us to go in to the station. Mum said she would call them while James and I headed off to parkrun.

It was a perfect day for running. We walked the mile or so to the park and milled around waiting for the Run Director's briefing. We both saw a couple of people that we knew, so did brief introductions to them and had a quick chat. After the briefing we lined up ready to start and we were off.

It was perfect conditions to run today. There was virtually no breeze and some sunshine, but it wasn't yet too warm. I didn't feel fantastic after my broken night's sleep so we had a gentle jog round chatting all the way. On the last lap I could see that James wanted to go faster so I suggested that he go ahead. He didn't want to initially but then changed his mind and upped his pace. I kept to the same pace and finished in just over 31 minutes. I was really pleased with that as I hadn't been going for a quick time. I really enjoyed the run and there was this really cute little lad running with his Mum nearby. I could hear them chatting and laughing most of the way round. On the final lap once James had disappeared, I heard them playing 'I spy', so I and another lady also joined in the game with

48

them. It was fun and the last lap flew by. Once I'd finished I introduced myself to the little lad who was called Josh and was 8 years old, and his Mum who was called Rachel. One of the nicest things about parkrun is the community of people who regularly attend and making new friends with them.

James walked me back home and popped in to see what the police had said to Mum. They made a record of what had happened during the night but also informed us that two other complaints of the same problem had been received nearby. That led them to believe the culprits were bored teenagers. They said they didn't have the resources to do any additional investigation at this time but if it happened again they would look into it further. They had at least provided Mum with a case number but did not require us to do a statement at a police station for the moment. Mum had also explained what happened to James last night, but as she wasn't there they couldn't do anything about it. They said for James & I to go to the police station if we wanted to take it further. We had actually discussed this on the walk back from parkrun and decided not to proceed with any further action.

James asked what I was doing this afternoon as we had originally discussed going to the lido together. I explained that Mum and I were now busy as we were heading over to see my aunt as it was her birthday. James had planned to meet up with Harry tonight so after checking that they were happy for Molly & I to gate-crash their night, we arranged to meet up at 8pm at the new bar (called Charlie's) that had opened up at the other end of the town.

Mum and I had a nice afternoon with Aunt Meg. It was her 58th birthday and we had bought her a spa day for her birthday. Mum & Aunt Meg had the spa day booked for a couple of weeks' time and it was lovely to see how excited Aunt Meg was. She had only been to a spa once before, so was very much looking forward to the outing. We had baked a chocolate cake for her birthday so we spent most of the afternoon drinking tea and eating. It was nice and chilled out.

Chapter 11

By the time we got home and had tea it was gone 7 o'clock so I only had a short time to get changed and head out to Charlie's to meet up with James, Harry & Molly. I was excited to go and still getting that butterflies feeling when I thought about James. I told Mum I was staying at Molly's afterwards, but actually I was hoping that James would invite me to stay at his.

In lieu of the occasion (at least it was an occasion in my head), I put on a summer dress that I had borrowed from Molly. It was white, floaty and made me feel both sexy and elegant which I hoped was a good combination. Mum thought it looked great and actually lent me a cardigan that I could wear with it. It was warm enough to not need a coat now, but later on it was likely to be chilly. I had arranged to meet up with Molly a few minutes early for a bit of a catch up before the boys arrived, so I walked into the bar at 7.45pm. Pretty record time to get ready and walk into town. I glanced around and saw Molly at a table in the far corner. It was the last table that had been free so we felt lucky to get it. As it was opening night, waiters and waitresses walked around with free champagne – well, free cava anyway. Anything free is always a bonus, so we helped ourselves.

I sat down with Molly and we had a quick catch up. She had a gameplan. She was going to hope that Harry invited her back to their flat, but if not, she was going to suggest that he came back to hers. Obviously, I didn't have that option so I was just hopeful that James would invite me back to his. As we chatted, Molly received a text from Harry explaining that he was late and it would be around 30 minutes before he arrived. We weren't bothered at all as it gave us a chance to catch up more.

I told Molly about the broken window and also about parkrun this morning. She asked how I was feeling about James. I said that I was excited because everything seemed to be going really well. I hoped that that would continue to be the case. It had been a while since we had both been happy with our partners at the same time, so it was exciting that things were working out for us. It was also ideal that Harry & James were best mates too. I asked Molly if James was with Harry too – we assumed this was the case as he had not turned up either.

It was nearly 40 minutes later that Harry strolled into the bar. He looked very relaxed & happy wearing a white shirt with the sleeves rolled up.

"Evening girls," remarked Harry. "How are you both? Have you had a good day?"

"Great thanks," we said simultaneously. "Where's James?" I added.

"I've no idea" replied Harry. "I had assumed he was already here with you."

It turned out that Harry hadn't heard from James all day. The last time he had seen him was when James was setting out for parkrun to meet me. When Harry had returned from his final rugby training session, it had been nearly 8 o'clock. They had stayed for a few drinks in the bar at the rugby club as it was the last session of the year. They now had a break for the summer and would reconvene in September.

Molly asked when I had last heard from James.

"Not since he left me this morning after parkrun. I don't know what he was doing today, but he just said he'd meet us here at 8pm".

I asked Harry if this was usual of James. Certainly from my experience James had always been very attentive and communicative so I was shocked that he hadn't turned up as planned. Harry was totally surprised, and said that this was completely out of character for him.

Where on earth was he? I initially felt a little angry as it seemed he had stood me up. But then it was such surprising behaviour that I felt worried. Had something perhaps happened to him? I asked Harry if he had walked here from their flat, but he'd got a taxi as he was running so late. So maybe something had happened to James? It was unlikely, but it was a possibility.

Harry picked up his phone and called James but it went straight through to his answerphone. Harry left him a message asking where he was. He then went to the bar to get us a round of drinks.

Molly and I chatted through the possibilities. Could he just be late? No – it was gone 9pm now. Could he have been attacked or something happened to him while walking here? I'd be surprised as it was evening, still light, and we hadn't heard about anything happening locally. Town was busy and we hadn't heard of any disturbances. Could he have forgotten? Impossible. We only talked about it this morning. It really was difficult to know what to think. I decided to send him a text message. Short and sweet.

Where are you? Are you coming?

But I didn't get a reply. And neither did Harry. Harry was just as puzzled as I was.

I stayed for another hour hoping that James would rock up full of apologies. But that didn't happen. No James, no text, no call, no excuses. Just nothing. It put a complete dampener on the evening for all of us. I decided to head home and Molly & Harry said they would walk back to his & James's house to see if they could find him. It was only 10pm so was just getting dark. I felt happy enough walking home on my own as there were streetlights on and enough people milling around.

I gave Molly & Harry a hug goodbye and left. As I walked past the chip shop I debated stopping for some cheesy-chips, but decided against it. I wasn't really hungry. Just a bit sad – and a bit worried. When I was just around the corner from home, I was on my own for the first time. There were no more people around me. I thought I heard someone behind me, but when I turned abruptly there was nobody there. I sped up. Again, I thought I heard footsteps and turned quickly. But I couldn't see anyone. I was probably imagining it. I was a little freaked out from the events of the past 24 hours and then upset from James not arriving. I hugged my arms around me and ran the rest of the way home. Mum's house was a welcoming sight. As I ran into the garden I breathed a sigh of relief. I stopped on the doorstep and turned around – but there was no-one there. I let myself in and found Mum in the kitchen with the kettle boiling.

Mum made us both a cup of tea and asked me how my evening was. She was surprised to see me as she hadn't expected me back at all tonight. I texted Molly to let her know I had got home ok, and to see if they had seen any sign of James on their way home. She replied that they were only halfway back but hadn't seen anything. Everything was quiet with no evidence of any disturbances.

She said she would text again once they got back to Harry's flat. I updated Mum on the fact that James had just not turned up. She was surprised as she had seen how keen James had appeared to be. She seemed more concerned that something might have happened to him than thinking that he'd just stood me up. The fact that he hadn't been in touch with Harry either was just odd. I really didn't know what to think and I didn't feel like going to bed just yet.

Fifteen minutes later Molly texted again to say that they'd arrived home but the flat was empty. Harry couldn't tell if James had been home that day or not. James's bedroom was very tidy which was apparently always the case. It would be unusual for him to leave clothes on the floor apparently and whilst there were some dishes in the dishwasher he couldn't remember what had been in there that morning. Harry still hadn't had a response from James either. Molly was going to stay with Harry tonight, so she promised that as soon as James turned up she would let me know.

I couldn't imagine I was going to sleep much that night, but in the end, I slept surprisingly well. It was nice to be back in my own bed (the window had been replaced) and I had been really tired from the events of the previous night. So I slept right through until 7am. At that point I texted Molly to see if they had heard from James as the last text received at 1am had just said:

Nothing to report. Good night.

I jumped out of bed and decided to make Mum and I a Full English breakfast. If nothing else, it would take my mind off James' no-show at least for a short time. I was gathering together the eggs, bread, sausages and hash browns when a text pinged through. It was from Molly:

Still no news yet. He's not come home. I will call you in a couple of hours.

By the time breakfast was cooked, Mum had come down and made a pot of tea. We sat together and tucked in to our food. I explained that James still hadn't turned up and I wasn't sure whether to be angry or worried.

"He really seemed very keen on you," said Mum.

"I thought so too," I replied. "But maybe that's how he is with people? Maybe he appears really keen but actually it's a bit of a front, and he's not that keen after all."

"I'm sure there will be a sensible explanation. Maybe he went somewhere and forgot to take a phone charger," suggested Mum.

"Maybe, I'm giving him the benefit of the doubt for the moment, but there had better be a good explanation".

My phone started to ring. It was Molly.

"Hi Lily, how are you?" asked Molly

"I'm fine," I replied "Other than completely confused and not sure whether to be angry or worried. Have you heard from him?"

"We are completely confused too. James still hasn't come home and Harry hasn't heard from him either. We just don't know what to think" exclaimed Molly.

"Should we go to the police and report him as a missing person?" I suggested. "Or contact his parents or other friends perhaps?"

"Harry doesn't want to worry his parents unnecessarily as we don't know for sure that he is missing. He is a grown adult after all, and just hasn't been in touch. Harry is happy to give them a call later though and see if they have heard from him. Maybe there was a family emergency and he had to go home and didn't get a chance to let us know?" Molly mused.

"I think adults have to be missing for at least 24 hours for the police to take any act……,"

"Hold on, Lily" interrupted Molly. I heard murmurings between Molly and James.

"Harry has just had a text from James. He's fine. He said he's sorry and will call you later to explain things".

"Where is he?" I asked.

"No idea" stated Molly. "That's all the text says".

We discussed the text message and what could have happened further, but we were really only speculating as we had no further information. On the one hand, at least we knew that James was ok. On the other hand, I'm furious that he's been incommunicado and stood me up. I arranged to give Molly a call later when I knew more. She also said she'd let me know if they hear back from James again.

I turned back to my breakfast which was now on the cool side. I was too annoyed to finish it, so I picked at a sausage and bit of hash brown and then chucked the rest of it in the bin. I brought Mum up to speed with the text message and the fact that James was at least safe.

"Well that's a good thing of course. I'm glad he's safe. Now we just need an explanation for what happened and why he didn't turn up as planned last night" said Mum.

"Exactly," I agreed. "And it had better be a good one."

I was at a bit of a loose end this morning. There were plenty of things that I could do, but I just wanted to hear from James.

I heard the chime of a text on my mobile. I dived towards it hoping it was James.

Fancy a drink one night this week?

It was from an unknown number, but I recognised the number so I knew exactly who it was. It was from Rob. I had deleted his number so that I wasn't tempted to message him. But now was not the time. I wanted to hear from James, not Rob. I decided just to ignore his message and hope that he left me alone.

Finally I decided to go for a walk. And to leave my mobile at home. At least that way I would stop staring at it willing it to ring. I set out around a local circuit with very beautiful scenery. But today, so many thoughts were rushing through my head and I didn't really take in the swans with the cygnets, the birds twittering in the trees and the rabbits scurrying in the hedgerows.

When I returned I reached for my phone. There was a text. And it was finally from James.

I'm sorry for last night. Can you meet me at 4pm at the bridge in the park so that I can explain?

I wasn't sure in which tone to reply really. I was so confused. So I just replied with a very simple

Yes.

Chapter 12

James and I met up in the park by the bridge. It was part of the parkrun course, so we were both very familiar with it. It was usually quiet, it was pretty – it was a good place to chat without being overheard. When I strolled up James was already there – sitting on the bridge with his legs hanging off the side. He was breaking up and throwing small sticks into the stream. It was a lovely day so we were both dressed casually in shorts.

"Hi," I said as I approached him.

"Hi, I'm sorry" was his reply. He scrambled up to stand beside me. "Shall we walk?" he asked.

"Yes, that's a good idea" I confirmed.

Walking gave me something to do with my hands and arms whilst nervously waiting for him to speak.

"I'm not really sure where to start," said James.

"Just start from the beginning," I countered.

"So, I left you yesterday morning and went back to the flat. As soon as I walked in I received a call from my ex-girlfriend. The one that moved to the US if you remember?" started James.

"Wasn't that two years ago?" I squeaked. No idea why my voice had gone so high.

"Yes, that's right. She went to live with her dad. Well, she's back visiting some family and wanted to say hi, and catch up".

"OK…." I said. I wasn't sure that I liked where this was going.

"So I met up with Jazz – her proper name is Jasmine – and we went for a walk and then a coffee. She asked how I was and what I had been up to. I explained that I was living with Harry now and that I had a new girlfriend.

I told her that I was happy, and asked what she had been up to."

I was starting to feel more apprehensive. His voice was slowing down and he was obviously finding it hard to tell me this.

"So, when Jazz moved to live with her dad, she worked as a nurse in the local hospital. She was intending to stay there permanently, but now her dad has a new girlfriend that she is not that keen on. She wants to come back here to live. She wants to get back together with me."

I could have guessed this was going to happen. James really was a special kind of guy. I'm not surprised that she wanted him back. And there are always nurse vacancies available here, so it wouldn't be difficult for her to get a job.

James looked at me.

"I'm really sorry I didn't contact you last night. I was totally thrown by this. I just didn't know what to say or do so I just buried my head in the sand." said James.

"Were you with Jasmine last night? Did you stay with her?" I asked.

"Goodness no," replied James. "Of course not. I was just so confused. I went to stay with my brother who lives an hour away. I just needed some space to think about things."

I heaved a sigh of relief. Well that was something. At least I didn't have to picture him rolling around in bed with another girl all night.

"So what are you going to do? Is she back already? Where is she living?" I asked. So many questions.

"No, she's going back to the States on Monday. But she's applied for some jobs and is hoping to be back for good in two to three weeks' time. She's going to stay with her Mum for a month or so until she gets her first pay packet, and then she is looking to rent a flat nearby."

"And how do you feel? Do you want to get back with her?" I held my breath awaiting his answer.

"Well, I was happy with you. I know it was early days, but we get on great. I was having fun. Now, I'm all confused. I was with Jazz for 18 months before she moved away. That's quite a lot of history. But it seems like a long time ago now. I wasn't sure how I felt when I was with her yesterday. I was pleased to see her, and I certainly care for her a lot. But I'm not sure that getting back with her is the right thing to do, or what I want to do" explained James.

"Is her coming back here conditional on getting together with you, or is she coming back anyway?" I asked.

"She's coming back anyway. She has lots of friends here, she has some family here. She doesn't want to be in Florida anymore. She's had enough of the threat of guns and the way of life in the US. Plus she doesn't like her dad's new girlfriend very much."

I could understand the situation that James is in. I was happy that he was being open and talking to me about things – even if I didn't really like hearing them. Apart from not letting me know that he wasn't coming out last night, he had behaved like a total gentlemen. Still, I needed to let him know that how he handled last night was not acceptable.

"I was really worried about you last night. So was Molly & Harry. We even thought you might have been attacked, beaten up or run over", I said. "We had no idea what had happened to you. And you never came home or let any of us know that you were ok. That was really out of order".

"You are absolutely right. And I'm really sorry about that," James responded. "I fully intended to contact you, but my phone ran out of juice, I hadn't taken a charger with me, and my brother has a different type of phone. I didn't know your or Harry's number off-by-heart and so I couldn't think of a way to get hold of you. I was going to call the pub, but then had a few beers with my brother and totally forgot to do so. I am sorry for worrying you, and I will apologise to Harry and Molly too".

"So what are you going to do?" I questioned. It seemed to me that James had some decisions to make. I wanted to carry on seeing him and it appeared that Jasmine also wanted to get back with him. The ball was definitely in his court.

"To be honest," remarked James. "It's difficult. You and I are great together and I've absolutely loved the last few weeks getting to know you. We've had great fun together, you are funny, gorgeous, caring – you tick all my boxes. And it seems like such a long time ago that I was with Jazz. I don't really know her that well now. We had a good relationship back when she was here before, but then she left, and although it took me a long time to move on, I did move on, and I was happy. I'm not sure that going back is the right thing to do. Especially when I'm having fun with you."

"Well, I guess you have to figure out what you want. Do you want to get together in the next couple of days?" I asked.

"I was hoping that we could get together in a few days' time. Give me a little time to try and figure things out. Perhaps we could go out on Wednesday?" proposed James.

"That works for me. Let's go with that plan," I responded.

By this point we were back to our starting point, so I bid James farewell and headed home. Whilst walking back I called Molly and gave her a brief update on what had happened with James.

"Come out for a drink with just me tonight," she suggested. "We can have a girly catch up."

"Perfect," I agreed. "See you at the pub around the corner from Mum's at 7pm."

When I got home Mum was out. So I just sent her a text message with a quick explanation to the situation with James. It saved me going through it all again so I was quite pleased.

A little later I walked into the pub and Molly was already waiting. She already had a pint of cider waiting for me and was sitting at a table in the corner so that we had some privacy. I brought Molly up to speed with a detailed account of what James had said and the current dilemma that he was facing.

"It's obvious that James really likes you," mused Molly. "He's really into you. You can see from the way that he looks at you, the way that he laughs with you and the way that his face lights up every time you walk into a room - and every time that you are talking with him."

"Well that's nice to hear, thank you," I responded. "However, he very much has unfinished business with Jasmine. He was obviously gutted when she left, and took a long time to get over her…"

"Yes, maybe, but he did get over her. And he moved on" countered Molly. "I really think he just needs a bit of time to figure things out. Have you slept with him yet?"

"No, which I'm glad about now. If we'd got that far down the road it would have been really gutting if he then left me for his ex," I stated.

We carried on speculating for a while, and then I asked Molly about her and Harry.

"Everything is great thanks. We really click. The more I spend time with him, the more that I like him," she explained.

"And did you sleep with Harry last night?" I asked.

"Yep," she replied. "And it was fantastic. We didn't get to sleep very much. We were quite inventive and got to know each other's likes and dislikes fairly well" she laughed. "I'm really tired now and am looking forward to a decent night's sleep in my own bed tonight."

"I'm really pleased for you," I said. "You so deserve someone nice after having been single for quite a while. And Harry seems really good for you. The two of you definitely click. I'm really happy for you".

"Oh, I know what I forgot to ask," interrupted Molly. "Have you heard any more from Rob?".

That reminded me. I had totally forgotten about his text a couple of days back in all the recent drama. I wasn't sure if I should be replying to him or not. Molly seemed to think that I should ignore Rob – assuming that I was no longer interested in him – and see if he went away. That was my opinion at this point too. I was still a bit freaked out by the fight in the pub and the rock through the window. Of course, both incidents could be nothing to do with Rob – but equally, there was a small chance that it could be Rob causing trouble.

We spent the next hour or so chatting amicably before heading home for an early night and a bit of soul searching for me.

Chapter 13

I woke up with a jump in the midst of a bad dream. I'd been holding James's jumper pulling hard on his arm, and Jasmine had been pulling hard on his other arm. It was like playing tug-of-war with a human. Poor James was stuck in the middle being pulled in both directions at the same time. I yawned and stretched, already debating in my head about what was going to happen.

I really cared about James, even though it had only been a short time that we had been together. Jasmine had been with him much longer, but then left when she went to the US. He told me himself that it had taken a long time for him to get over it – in fact I was the first person he had properly dated in the two years since she had left. Maybe that shared history would be more important to him. I could understand the situation that James was in. It must be hard for him.

The week stretched ahead. I had nothing planned until seeing James on Wednesday. I wasn't looking forward to going to work, but in the end Monday flew by as it usually does. As I was leaving the office Monday evening, I was tapped on the arm. I turned around and it was Rob.

"Come and have a coffee with me – please?" he asked.

I thought quickly. I didn't want to appear rude, or say no & anger him, but it would be quite useful to talk to Rob and see if he had been out the night that James got punched. So I agreed that I would join him just for a quick coffee.

66

We went into a nearby café and Rob queued to get a coffee for him and a tea for me. At least he remembered that I don't like coffee. I settled down at a small table in the window so that we had a little privacy but were also highly visible.

"How are you? I mean really?" asked Rob.

"I'm fine thanks. I've been keeping busy," I replied.

"What have you been up to?" he queried.

"I've been running a bit, a few nights out with Molly, just bits and pieces really," I explained. "How about you?"

"Nothing really, just working, rowing, hanging out with a few mates," he answered. "I went away to see some friends in Manchester last weekend."

"Really? I didn't know you had friends in Manchester," I responded.

"You don't know everything about me you know. I've been making an effort to catch up with old friends recently," he said.

Have you been out in town at all?" I asked.

"Nope, you know town isn't my thing really," Rob said.

So he says that he hasn't been in town which theoretically rules him out of the brawl in the pub last week. Especially if he was telling the truth about going to Manchester, and although he's not always behaved very well, he doesn't particularly have a habit of lying.

"Did you like the flowers that I sent?" he asked.

"You only ever once got me flowers in all the time that we were together. Why now?" I queried.

"Maybe I took you for granted somewhat. I feel like I didn't treat you as well as I should have when we were together. It's an easy mistake to make. We should have talked about it, rather than ended things between us" Rob explained.

"You never wanted to talk about things. You never talked to me. And you didn't let me have a life. You kicked off every time I wanted to see my friends – even though you were invited too. It's not like I ever said that it was girls only – and you couldn't ever come" I retorted.

"But they were single. I was the only guy. It's weird being there as your partner when the others were all single girls," said Rob.

"Hmmm, but then you stopped me going with them. I hardly ever got to see my friends," I complained. "I just think maybe we are at different stages of our lives. As you are a little bit older than me, you were more inclined to settle down and were happy just to stay in or do things on our own. I need a social life. I need friends around me. I still need to have some fun".

"It's called being mature – and a grown up," Rob huffed. "You should try it sometime".

I stood up, said thank you for the tea and that I was leaving. I just didn't see the point in continuing this conversation.

"Wait," pleaded Rob. "Stay – I'm sorry, I didn't mean to be rude".

"You never do," I replied. "I'll see you around".

I left the café feeling frustrated. It didn't seem like he knew anything about the brawl in the pub, or the rock through the window – not that I had specifically mentioned either incident of course. I thought he might have followed me away from the coffee shop, but luckily he didn't. I turned around a few times whilst walking home, but there was nobody there.

I did get the odd text from James over the next couple of days, but they didn't give much insight into his thoughts. The dynamics of our relationship certainly seems to have changed. I wasn't sure that I was looking forward to Wednesday, because although I was keen to see him, I didn't want to hear any bad news.

Wednesday morning came, and whilst I was showering I received a text.

Can I take a rain check on tonight please? I will call you in the next few days and arrange something else. Thanks. James.

Great. So that left me precisely nowhere. I felt frustrated, like I was stuck going round in circles and couldn't move forwards. I decided that I would do my best to not get wound up, and just leave things for a few days. On the plus side, not going out would enable me to save up a little money. By avoiding nights out and not having any rent to pay, I was managing to save quite a bit. This would enable me to move quicker back into my own place in a few months' time.

The week went by, I didn't hear anything else from James, and even Molly was going away with Harry this weekend so I didn't really have anyone to go out with on Friday. Mum and I stayed in with a takeaway and a movie instead. We watched Bridget Jones's Baby which is a great film that I have seen before but would always be happy to watch it again. I feel quite balanced after watching Bridget Jones' films as she seems to be in a permanent state of chaos.

Chapter 14

Saturday morning dawned bright and early. The sun was out, it was a nice warm temperature again – and it was parkrun day. I had actually been for a few runs this week, so I was feeling well prepared for a good go at my previous personal best. It's always very satisfying to get a new PB, and I knew that if I managed it I would be on a high all weekend.

I was also very nervous as I didn't know if James would be at parkrun or not. I guess he knew there was a good chance that I would go, so if he didn't want to see me he was unlikely to be there. Equally, it would give him an opportunity to bump into me if he wanted to.

I arrived nice and early, giving me time to chat to a few people that I was now starting to recognise from previous occasions. The girl wearing the skort with a bright pink t-shirt that I ran with for a while last time. The cute guy that I had spotted a couple of times before – although both times I'd been with James so hadn't really taken any notice other than a quick smile. The oldish guy that reminded me of a younger version of my grandfather (who unfortunately passed away when I was in my early teens). The dad that pushed a double buggy with two little kids that could only have been 1 or 2 years old. There wasn't any sign of James though. He was always very punctual, so it was highly unlikely that he was coming. I felt really disappointed, but had spotted a couple of glances from the cute guy. Well, I thought he was looking at me anyway. It's always quite hard to tell when you are in a crowd of people.

We all gathered around for the parkrun briefing carried out by the Run Director. Amidst the jostling, I suddenly found myself next to the cute guy who was about 6 feet tall, dark hair, a gleaming smile and a dimple in his cheek that gave him the real 'boy next door' look. He looked directly at me, gave me a big smile, and introduced himself with a whisper as Jack.

As we made our way to the start line, Jack and I exchanged a few pleasantries. I told him that I was going for a PB today and he offered to pace me – but I declined. I really just wanted to run for myself this week. At least that way I could back off if I chose to without the added pressure of trying to look good in front of a cute guy. Jack said that he was recovering from an injury so would be running a steady 23 minutes. I laughed – how can anyone call 23 minutes steady?

5-4-3-2-1-parkrun – and we were off. The slight delay at the start only lasted 3 or 4 seconds this week, so I must have started further forwards than normal. That did appear to be the case as loads of people streamed past me. I waved goodbye as Jack set off at pretty much twice my speed. It felt that way in any case.

Around 1km into the run, just as everyone had spread out and settled down into their normal pace, I realised that I was running next to Rachel and young Josh. It was lovely to see them both and we had a quick chat before I managed to pull away from them. I was definitely feeling stronger than on previous occasions. I actually was starting to feel like a real runner. It makes a big difference finding the time to do an extra couple of runs during the week – plus being hangover free is always an added bonus.

We set out on the 2nd lap and I was still feeling strong. I decided that if I still felt good on the 3rd and final lap I would try to increase the pace just a little more. By this time I was starting to overtake a few people that had set off too fast and had now drastically slowed down. I fixed my glance on a person with a particularly vibrant top maybe 30 feet in front of me, and vowed that I would try to overtake them. A couple of minutes later I had managed to pull level and then picked the next person to try to catch up. This really seemed to help me focus and concentrate on things other than the fact that MY LEGS WERE STARTING TO HURT.

I set out on the 3rd and final lap realising that whilst my legs were now hurting, my chest was also now hurting. I felt like I was pushing much harder than I had pushed before. I decided to abandon the idea of upping my pace as I really didn't think I would maintain it all the way to the end. Up until now my second lap had always been much slower than my first, but I had managed to keep up my initial pace this week. Half way round the last lap I took a glance at my watch and it said 22 minutes. Surely that wasn't right. Usually I was around 25 minutes at that point, I'm sure. I started to get excited attempting to calculate the maths in my head. I was definitely on for a PB – maybe even a good one? However, I was really starting to struggle now. I was glad I was on my own as there was no chance that I would have been able to hold a conversation with anyone. The hurt in my lungs had definitely overtaken the hurt in my legs now – although my legs were starting to feel rather jelly like. I worried briefly that I might actually collapse before the end, but suddenly I could sense that the finish was approaching. The penultimate corner, the last corner, cheers from those already at the finish. I pushed as hard as I could and managed to hold off another girl who was trying to overtake me. I ran over the line and nearly stumbled in the finish funnel pretty much barrelling headfirst into the lady giving out the finish tokens. Luckily I managed to save myself and not literally rugby tackle her to the ground. That could have been both painful and embarrassing. She gave me a beaming smile and handed me the token. I attempted to smile back but pretty sure it came out as more of a grimace with a bit of dribble and a runny nose. Lovely.

I took myself off to the side to recover and glanced at my watch. Of course, I'd forgotten to stop my trusty Garmin sports watch and it was still going – but it said 28 mins and 48 seconds. OMG – I had absolutely smashed my previous PB which was over 30 minutes. It must have been 28 mins and something.

As I stood to the side, chest heaving and on wobbly legs, Jack came up and congratulated me on my PB. He had clearly finished some time ago and had completely recovered. I on the other hand still couldn't breathe. Aside from feeling like a hot, sticky, red-faced mess, it was good to see him and I felt very proud. It was a few more seconds before I could speak and I was very excited. Jack seemed to soak up my excitement and told me that I'd done an amazing job. I couldn't wait for the times to be released later.

After being scanned and saying goodbye to Jack I started walking home. Jack had offered to walk me home but I declined as he lived in the opposite direction. I did however give him my phone number when he asked if he could message me later. I was still hoping that things would work out with James, but it was always good to have alternative options – and certainly Jack was a good looking option.

A couple of hours later a text pinged through from parkrun.

You finished today in a time of 28 minutes and 18 seconds. Congratulations on a new PB.

Wow. I was so excited and happy. What a buzz. I had absolutely smashed my previous time. The only downside was that it would now be really hard to beat that time again.

As I had a quiet day planned, I chilled out at home, took a walk around the block and then started looking into a half marathon to run later in the year. I had never run that distance before so it would be a massive challenge. I hadn't run over 5 miles for a long time, so would need to step up my training. I found a popular but scenic half marathon in September and decided that would be a good one to enter. It was a trail run which is something different that I hadn't experienced before. It wasn't very hilly but I would certainly need to practice running off-road and up some gentle hills. It would give me a nice challenge to focus on, and a reason to keep going out running and taking part in parkrun.

Sunday morning I received a text from James and arranged to meet him again in the park for a walk. After lunch I headed over, full of nerves and excited to see him again. It was a little awkward when we first met up. We had a hug but didn't kiss each other. We set out for our walk. I asked James how he was feeling.

"I'm still confused," he stated. "Jazz is back in the US at the moment but returns for good next weekend. She wants to meet up as soon as she is back here. I have explained to her the situation and told her that I'm happy to meet up as friends, but not to assume that we will get back together. I really need to figure out if that is what I want. I really appreciate that you have been brilliant about this – you've given me some space & time and not put any pressure on me. I'm really grateful about that".

"Well, it's difficult I have to admit" I levelled with him. "I really like you, and I've really enjoyed our time getting to know you. It was a total blow when you stood me up last weekend, but I do understand the dilemma you are in. I am relieved that you have been honest with me – many men would have lied to me and not told me the truth".

"Please rest assured that I have really enjoyed getting to know you too. That's why this is a hard decision. If I hadn't met you I would have jumped at the chance to get back with Jazz. I never wanted to split up with her in the first place, even though the relationship wasn't perfect, but that wasn't an option".

We continued to chat and walk. James reached out and held my hand which was nice. I have always felt so comfortable with James. I ended up telling him about meeting up with Rob. He was a little concerned for me, but I reassured him that Rob would now realise that I had no further interest in being with him.

"Even if we weren't together any longer?" asked James.

"Even then. I really have moved on and looking back makes me remember all the controlling behaviour and difficult times. I really have no interest in going back to that toxic relationship. I would much rather be single".

James asked if I went to parkrun this weekend. I told him all about my new PB and how delighted I was. I avoided mentioning meeting with Jack however. I didn't think he really needed to know about that. Well, there was nothing to know really. It was only a cute guy I had briefly chatted to, and I hadn't heard from him since. James pulled my hand to stop me, turned me towards him, and looked straight into my eyes.

"I'm so happy for you. It's such a great feeling when you manage a new PB".

My whole body tingled. He looked at my lips, and I looked at his. All I wanted was for James to bend down and kiss me – which he did. Very lightly, and very slowly. I felt sparks of electricity and he put his arms around me. We kissed long and hard and only broke apart when we heard someone say 'get a room' at us. We laughed. The tricky atmosphere between us had disappeared and I felt really comfortable again. James looked so much more relaxed and happy. We spent another hour walking together and then stopped for an ice-cream and lay down together next to the lake in the park. It was a beautiful afternoon and it was amazing to spend the time with James again.

We discussed our situation further and decided that we would see how things went over the next couple of weeks. James actually was working away during the week for the next two weeks so he wasn't going to be around very much anyway. He asked if I would mind if he saw Jazz one day next weekend – purely on a platonic basis. I did mind really, but said that I understood that he needed to do that to figure out his feelings.

I asked what Jazz was like. Was she sporty? Did they have lots in common? It turned out that Jazz was a bit like Molly – a bit more girly, not really into sports and she sounded a bit posher than me. Her parents were well off so sometimes they had gone to the theatre and some more glitzy types of events. That really wasn't my sort of thing, and I wouldn't have thought that James would be too keen either. He said that he really liked running and doing adventurous things with me, so I hoped that after spending some time with Jazz again he would decide to stick with me.

The next two weeks were going to be very hard though. I knew that I had to back off and give James some space to figure things out. It was going to be really difficult knowing that he was going to spend some time with Jazz too, but I did trust him enough to believe that he would finish things with me before moving on with her – if that was what he chose to do. He had told me that he had never been unfaithful to a girlfriend before – and he had no intention of starting now. That made me feel slightly happier about the situation.

I told James about my half marathon plans. He loved the idea and wanted to sign up too. I asked him to leave it a while, because if he did decide that he wanted to be with Jazz it would put a really dampener on the event for me – and I didn't want that if I had spent the summer training. He was totally understanding and said that he would enter nearer the time if that was appropriate.

We had a lovely long kiss before saying goodbye and James walked me home. He always is such a gentleman, and I always feel so safe and secure when I'm with him. Even if he did get back with Jazz, I did hope that we would be able to stay friends – even though it would be difficult – and Jazz probably wouldn't be keen.

I didn't invite James in as it seemed simpler not to. Once he had left I chatted with Mum who had some news for me. Mum had been in town earlier and had bumped into Rob. She had tried to engage him in conversation but he apparently just hadn't been interested. I was hopeful that was a good sign and that he had accepted that we were well and truly over. Mum agreed and said that she thought that was indeed the case. We hadn't had any more incidents of any type and hopefully there wouldn't be any more in the future. Of course, I had no evidence that Rob was involved in either the brawl or the rock through the window, but as more time passed by I felt it less and less likely that he had been.

Chapter 15

The week trickled by. James was away working so I didn't see him – he was getting back Friday night but had a family engagement – it was his brothers birthday. Given the circumstances, he didn't feel that inviting me along was appropriate, so I was at a loose end. I gave Molly a call and she suggested a girls night out, but I really wasn't interested. We decided to go swimming instead. This week the weather had got hotter and hotter – and Friday was due to be the hottest day before the heat wave broke over the weekend. We arranged to meet up straight after work at the lido. This is a heated, outdoor swimming pool in the nearby town. We don't go very often but it's always good fun when we do.

I arrived by 5.30pm and Molly was waiting outside the ticket kiosk for me. There was a stream of families leaving and a queue of teenagers waiting to enter. We joined the back of the queue and ten minutes later were changing into bikini's. It was so hot we planned to have a sunbathe before our first swim.

We found an area of grass with a couple of spare sunbeds and made our base. First stop was then the ice-cream shop. Whilst eating ice-cream we chatted together. Molly told me that she had stayed at Harry's most nights this week – they had made the most of James being away. I heard far too much detail about their shenanigans all around the boys' flat. I was not sure that I wanted to go there now – and I would certainly have reservations about sitting on the sofa or eating at the kitchen table....

James had messaged a couple of times. He was planning on meeting up with Jazz on Saturday and wanted to see me on Sunday. At least that meant that I could enjoy parkrun. I brought Molly up-to-date on my parkrun achievements last week and also mentioned meeting Jack. She laughed and asked if I was excited to see him again.

"Not really, he was cute, but I'm not in a position to take anything further right now as I'm more than hung up on James. I also haven't heard from him even though I gave him my phone number, so he's obviously not interested. It really was just a chat in the park with a cute guy – nothing further," I explained.

Molly asked if I would have replied if he had texted me.

"Of course I would. Things are so up in the air with James at the moment, and I have to accept that he needs to spend some time with Jazz. There is really no harm in my chatting to someone new. Not that I would let anything happen of course. I really wouldn't like to complicate the situation any further – it wouldn't be fair on anyone".

I had total respect for James, and despite the difficult situation, he had handled things in a respectful manner. So I had no intention of behaving inappropriately in any way.

I told Molly that if Jack did contact me I would be completely up front with him about the situation I am in. I was planning on going to parkrun again in the morning and I knew that James wouldn't be there this week. So I was hoping that Jack would be. If nothing else, it would take my mind off things.

Molly and I spent the next half an hour in the water. It was scorching hot and lovely to be in and out of the water without getting cold. We did a few lengths and then messed about in the shallow end. We had a handstand competition (which I won, mainly as Molly always holds her nose when she's under the water). It was a really pleasant evening and we stayed until 9pm when the lido closed. We debated going for a drink but neither of us really felt up for it, so we decided to part ways and go home for a quiet evening.

I'd had a good week running-wise. I did some research last weekend on increasing speed and had decided to do two or three additional runs each week including one with intervals. This is where you jog quietly to warm up and then run a series of fast stretches interspersed with slow recovery jogs before a steady cool down. From the reading that I had done it seems that this is the best way to improve your 5K times. I also was aware that I needed to try to fit in a weekly long run in preparation for my autumn half marathon. I need to gradually increase the mileage by maybe 1 extra mile per week until I get up to around 11 miles or so. This should be enough distance to make the half marathon in September achievable – and hopefully at a fairly good time. As I hadn't run a half marathon before, I didn't really have any idea what time I would aim for. But I do like to have a goal. However, as the half marathon that I had entered is off-road (which means that you have different terrains and undulations to consider) the time is likely to be significantly slower than road races. My aim however is to be finished in 2 hours 30 minutes or better.

I had executed my first interval session on Wednesday. It was an absolute killer. I thought I was going to collapse. I jogged to the park to warm up, and then did 2 minutes of fast running with 2 minutes of very steady jogging in between to recover. I repeated this 5 times. By the last interval I had to walk for a minute or so to recover after the fast work as I was absolutely exhausted. My legs went all wobbly and I had to walk before I keeled over. I soon recovered though and was then able to jog home. The next day my legs felt stiff – I could certainly tell that I had done something different. However, by Saturday I felt great and was hopeful to get another good run.

After a pleasant swim last night, and a nice bright start to Saturday morning, I walked quietly to parkrun hopeful of a good time and possibly a new PB. The changes to my running regime hopefully would be evident in a faster, stronger run today. However, you can never really tell how you are going to feel until you get going.

I arrived quite early and chatted easily to a few people that I was now starting to recognise. I waved to Rachel and her son Josh and kept an eye out for James – but I didn't see him at all. I couldn't see that Jack was here either which was rather disappointing. The run briefing started and my hopes were dashed – Jack obviously wasn't coming today. I hadn't realised quite how much I was looking forward to seeing him. Briefing over, everyone headed to the start line and suddenly I spotted Jack – arriving late. A smile broke over my face and my heart raced. I was surprised by the reaction that him arriving had on me. I saw him scanning the crowd as if he was looking for someone – and then he smiled as he spotted me. He headed straight towards me.

"Ah – how lovely to see you. I was hoping you'd be here," said Jack.

"Well, I have to admit that seeing you has brightened up my morning," I answered.

"So what's it to be today? Are you aiming for a PB?" asked Jack.

"That's the plan. I'm actually really nervous," I replied. I outlined the training that I had carried out this week and Jack reassured me that that would certainly help. The countdown began and we were off. Jack started jogging beside me.

"Please go on ahead – I don't want to hold you up," I suggested.

Jack was adamant that he was happy to run with me. He said that he'd been having some niggles with a previous injury so was planning on a steady run in any case. So he offered to pace me to a 28 minute PB. I wasn't confident that I could do that, but I was certainly willing to try.

It was a lovely morning for running again. Still fairly cool at the moment but was going to be hot this afternoon. There was just a little breeze and it was nice and bright. As we ran together I could hear snippets of conversation from other people. Everyone seemed to be in a bright and cheerful mood. It's amazing how a nice morning and a jog with friends sets you up for a good day.

By the second lap I was still feeling pretty strong and hopeful that I'd be able to up the pace slightly next time around. Jack remarked that if we stayed at this pace we would meet our target of 28 minutes. As the third and final lap came around I started to struggle. Jack continued to chat but wasn't getting any response from me now. I was having to use all my breath and energy to keep my legs moving at this pace. As we came to the penultimate corner Jack encouraged me to sprint for the finish. I could hardly breathe now and was pumping my arms to try and kid my legs into running just that little bit faster. As the finish funnel came into view I dug deep and pushed as hard as I could. Yet another near collapse over the finish line into the funnel and gasping for breath as I took the finish token from the volunteer with an attempt at a smile. I was elated. I had managed a sub-28 minutes. I wasn't quite sure what the official time would be but it was around 27 minutes 50 seconds. Of course, having Jack pacing me was extremely helpful and I had dug deep and tried my best.

I was effusive with my thanks – once I could speak. Jack was very pleased for me and I think I had impressed him with my efforts. What a great start to the weekend. Whilst we had been running Jack explained that he must have put my number wrong into his phone. He had tried to text me during the week but it was undeliverable. I checked the number that he had for me and there was indeed a digit missing. It was nice to know that he had tried to contact me.

We decided to go to a local café together for a celebratory breakfast. I was ecstatic about my run and was keen to get to know Jack a little more. Although I did want to explain about the situation that I was in.

Thirty minutes later we were tucking in to a full English with crispy bacon and no black pudding. I'm such a creature of habit. Jack asked me if I had a boyfriend. I took my time explaining the situation with James.

"So you have only been dating him a few weeks, and now you are having a break until he figures out if he wants to be with you?" he asked.

"That's pretty much the situation," I confirmed. "It's obviously very early days but with Jasmine reappearing James needs to figure out what he wants to do. In fact, he's spending the day with Jasmine today."

"And how do you feel about that?" asked Jack.

84

"Well, I was quite gutted, but all of a sudden I'm not so bothered now" I replied. And to my surprise, that was true. I was really enjoying spending some time with Jack and getting to know him a little bit.

Aside from Jack being very good looking, we did appear to have a good connection between us. There was definitely some chemistry. We chatted really easily and seemed to get along very well. I found Jack really interesting to talk to which is something that's very important to me. He seemed to be very knowledgeable and I could talk about pretty much any topic and he seemed well informed. During our run we had chatted a little about politics, about the environment, about music that we liked and our jobs. Jack had worked for the council for a number of years before setting up his own business as a tree surgeon. This involved some tree felling but more often tree maintenance work. He had some emergency jobs especially during and after extreme weather events such as major storms. The majority of his work was pruning or trimming back trees as well as felling unwanted trees or unblocking roads. He'd built up his business over the last two years and now even had an apprentice that worked for him.

In his spare time he liked to run, visit the gym and go hiking and climbing. He was in great physical shape and it was evident that Jack was the outgoing and adventurous type. The more I got to know him, the more I liked him. It was bizarre that I'd ended up meeting two guys that I liked.

Jack asked me if I wanted to go out with him this evening. Whilst I was tempted I didn't really feel like this was appropriate given the current situation with James. So I declined his invitation but did agree to meet up with him again tomorrow morning for a run. I knew I'd be waiting to hear from James and having something else to do would be a bonus. Jack had been quite understanding of the situation and didn't seem to be the type to play games.

Jack told me that next weekend he was going hiking in Snowdonia. He was heading off Friday and camping for a couple of nights. He was going with another couple of friends and suggested that I join him as well. It did sound like a fun opportunity and I hadn't been up Snowdon before, so I said that I would let him know once I'd found out if I could have Friday off of work. By early next week I should also know what was going on with James, so could decide if I wanted to go away or not. I seemed to recall from a news article that Snowdon had a name change recently, so I asked Jack if that was true. Apparently it is – it's official name now is the proper Welsh name which is 'Yr Wyddf' and the region previously called Snowdonia is now called 'Eryri'. The phonetic pronounciation of Yr Wyddf is 'Uhr-With-Va'.

After leaving Jack, I walked home alone, deep in thought. I had no plans for the afternoon and decided I would stay home and help Mum with some jobs in the garden. If it was hot enough I could spend a couple of hours working on my suntan. It was going to be a difficult afternoon, knowing that James was with Jasmine, and I couldn't think of anything I could do that would actually take my mind off things. I wasn't expecting to hear from James until Sunday morning and that seemed like a really, really long time away.

I was therefore very surprised when James turned up at 4pm. Mum discreetly disappeared into the house and left James and I to talk. I looked at him and my heart dropped. I was guessing that it wasn't good news that he had turned up. He looked nervous and was fidgeting. He also looked drop dead gorgeous.

My heart sank as James explained that he felt he should come and see me immediately after spending the day with Jazz. They'd gone to a boating lake and had had a few hours to chat. James explained that he'd really enjoyed spending the day with her and had felt really uncomfortable about the situation. His intention had never been to mess me around, but he felt like he wanted to get back with Jazz and see if they could rekindle their relationship. They had too much unfinished business and too much history for him to walk away from. I was absolutely devastated to hear that he'd wanted to kiss Jazz all afternoon, and had only avoided doing so because we were still technically together and he didn't want to be disrespectful to me. It was a real blow to hear this, especially as all I wanted was to put my arms around him and pull him towards me for a kiss.

I could feel my emotions welling up inside me. James was such a decent guy, and I really couldn't fault how he had behaved. He'd been open and communicative with me – he'd been fair and refrained from kissing Jazz again until he'd given me the boot. However, now it was time for him to leave. I was only going to break down in front of him and make an utter fool of myself.

"I'm sorry Lily," said James. "I really didn't mean to hurt you. And I'd like to stay friends if we can?"

"Just go James. I just need you to go now please. I need to be by myself" I requested.

James stepped backwards and walked towards the garden gate. He left with the parting promise to call me in a couple of weeks.

As soon as he disappeared around the corner I started to cry. I'm not usually the crying type but the last few weeks had been such an emotional time. I'd felt so happy to meet James and spend time with him. And now, that was over. I felt like I was losing a friend as much as a boyfriend and that hurt a lot. I can't imagine that Jasmine and I would ever be friends so I couldn't really see that I would see much of James in the future. It had been so nice having someone to double date with Molly and I was sad that that opportunity was over. I'd only been with James a short time but it had been really fun – and full of promise. Now that hope was dashed. I often think that giving up on our hopes and dreams for a relationship is actually harder than giving up on the person themselves.

The rest of the day was spent eating ice-cream and watching films. It was definitely time for Bridget Jones again. It seemed strangely reassuring to watch Bridget launching from one disaster to the next. At least I wasn't the only one having relationship problems. On the other hand, at least I was lucky to have Jack on the horizon. It certainly made breaking up with James rather more palatable. It also gave me something to look forward to – I would be able to go on the camping/hiking trip next weekend now, assuming I could get Friday off work.

Chapter 16

It was yet another nice morning on Sunday. I felt really clear headed when I woke up, and then the events of yesterday flooded back. I felt a little sad knowing that James and I had broken up, but then on the plus side, I was looking forward to my run with Jack. We'd arranged to meet in the park at 10am. It was very hot and humid and the weather was due to break later – but not until this evening.

As I walked into the park, I immediately smiled at seeing Jack waiting for me. He really did have a hot body and a great smile. I automatically perked up and was looking forward to spending some time with him.

"Morning Lily, you are looking good today," commented Jack.

"Well thank you. You're not so bad yourself either," I replied.

"Are you up for running about 7km?" asked Jack. "I have a lovely route that I'd like to show you."

I agreed with the proviso that we stayed at a nice steady pace.

We started off as I had guessed by running around the lake in the park, but then we broke out over a stile at the far, quiet end of the park into a wood. It was a lovely path that I hadn't been down before. We wound quietly down into a very secluded area filled with the most wonderful bluebells. It actually looked like a lake there was so many of them. It was absolutely stunning.

The path continued to meander through the woods – much of the path was in the shade so we weren't getting too hot. We had a lovely chat about all sorts of things whilst running together – and we stayed at a nice, comfortable pace. My running had really been improving over the last few weeks so I was able to enjoy both the running & chatting with Jack.

"So are you up for the trip away next weekend?" asked Jack.

"Yes, as long as I can get Friday off work. Which hopefully shouldn't be a problem" I responded.

I brought Jack up to speed on the latest with James and confirmed that we were no longer together. He seemed quite understanding about the situation. He explained that he was going away with his best mate and his girlfriend – they are called Declan & Annie. They were leaving early Friday morning and would be camping until Sunday morning. They planned to do some hiking, a little bit of scrambling and some chilling out. Jack explained that scrambling is like going up and down mountains but where you don't need actual climbing ability, ropes or harnesses. It's more like using hands and legs to scramble up/down steep slopes. It sounds a bit scary, but I do like a bit of adventure, so I'm happy to go for it. Jack has promised to look after me…….

The week flew by and in no time at all we were off on our adventure. It was 6am when I was picked up. Declan was driving with Jack in the passenger seat, leaving Annie and I sat in the back. I was made to feel really welcome and the journey (in an old, slightly battered Land Rover) was quite comfortable and a good laugh. Declan was Irish – I really should have guessed this from the name – and had the typical Irish craic. I really warmed to him. Annie was a very petite, pretty girl with long, black, straight hair. She looked fit, strong and lean. Declan & Annie had been together for around 6 months, and seemed pleased that Jack had brought me along.

By early afternoon we had arrived in the Snowdon area. We were staying in a small campsite which was owned by the parents of one of Declan's friends. Jack had a 4-man tent which I would be sharing with him, and Declan had a 3-man tent which he & Annie would be sharing. Luckily I already had a sleeping bag and the boys had brought the rest of the equipment that we needed. We spent a pleasant couple of hours laughing and joking as we put up the tents, gathered firewood and built a fire. Jack had brought along a portable stove and a kettle so we were well set for a pleasant few days. I was pleased to see that there was a good shower & toilet block for us to use.

By 7pm we had cooked some burgers and hotdogs, we'd cracked open some beers & ciders and were all relaxing in front of the campfire. After a few cans had been consumed by each of us we recounted scary stories. I wasn't sure how much of them were fact, and how much was greatly exaggerated or entirely fictional, but all the same we had a good time.

Around 9 pm it had just turned dark and we were all feeling tired. We wanted to get a fairly early start in the morning so decided to head to bed. After cleaning my teeth I climbed into my sleeping bed and snuggled up next to Jack. We continued to chat together for a while, asking questions about family, work, relationships – just the usual getting to know each other. Despite being in a sleeping bag, lying just on a gym mat, I was fairly comfortable. As I was starting to drift off to sleep Jack looked straight into my eyes, and came closer for a kiss. It was a really slow, leisurely kiss. It started off with just lips and then I felt his tongue edge lightly into my mouth. Jack was a great kisser and I felt incredibly relaxed and happy. The edges of sleep drifted away and I felt wide awake and a little horny.

We both wanted to take things slowly, and get to know each other more before more physical things started to develop, so we said good night to each other and I turned my back on Jack. He slung an arm around my waist and we lay together very comfortably until we drifted off to sleep.

Chapter 17

Despite not having slept in a tent for many years, I had a fabulous night's sleep and woke up about 6.30am feeling refreshed. Jack was already awake and murmured good morning to me. We came together for a kiss, and I didn't even think about morning breath for a second. The kiss turned into a number of very long kisses, and about 10 minutes later we came up for air. It was time to get up and make some breakfast.

Jack opened up the tent and we clambered out. It was an amazing morning – warming up already with a fresh layer of dew on the grass. Declan & Annie already had the camping stove going and were in the process of making hot drinks and frying some bacon. The sizzling bacon smelt absolutely delicious and my mouth started to water.

"Thanks guys," said Jack. "That's really kind of you to get the breakfast cooked."

"No problem," responded Declan. "We figured that you two might be a little busy." Both Declan & Annie were laughing and my cheeks started to blush.

"Nothing too heavy to report," laughed Jack. "It's extremely early days and I like to be a gentlemen. And, just to be clear, it's our turn to make breakfast tomorrow."

Declan & Annie both seemed happy with that arrangement.

We settled down together feasting on bacon sandwiches and cups of tea or coffee. I felt incredibly contented and excited, if a little nervous for the day's activities. Declan, Annie & Jack had all been scrambling in Snowdonia before so they knew what was coming. It was all new for me.

I asked if we had any actual climbing to do, and if we would need any ropes or specialist climbing equipment. I had seen some ropes, harnesses and other bits and pieces, but it had all stayed in the Land Rover. Apparently it had been decided that we would stick to a fairly tame route which shouldn't need this type of equipment.

As I asked for the actual route details, it was explained that we were going to go and do a loop of around 8km which included Tryfan called the Cwm Bochlwyd Loop. 8 km doesn't sound too hard, but of course I hadn't taken into account the elevation. I had heard of Tryfan before, but not the Loop that we would be completing.

After packing up our equipment and storing it safely in our tents, we set off. I was starting to get really nervous by this time. Whilst having some semblance of fitness, the others all seemed super-fit in comparison. Jack did reassure me that all would be ok but I was still a little scared.

For the next hour we headed steadily upwards. Much of the route could be walked, some required scrambling on hands and knees. At no point did I feel like I was actually going to fall, although Jack did make sure that he was right behind me every step of the way. Declan led us, Annie followed and I was third with Jack helping me and explaining exactly where to go. He encouraged me to take my time and to not necessarily worry about keeping up with Annie at all times.

We were nearing the top of a ridge when we decided to stop for a break. We all sat down and looked around at the view. It was absolutely sensational. We had only seen a few other people all morning, and the weather was perfect. There was a light breeze, blue skies and sunshine. It was much cooler at the higher altitude but only enough to need a jumper. Declan & Jack were both carrying rucksacks and out of one Declan pulled a box full of sandwiches. I was amazed at how hungry I was despite eating only a couple of hours ago. I guess that's what happens when you are walking & climbing. We all tucked in and shared the sandwiches and a couple of bottles of water.

We set off again and this time had a downhill scramble before heading back upwards over a place called Bristly Ridge. An hour or so later we were at the top of another ridge and I felt absolutely knackered – as well as completely exhilarated. We had one moment where I was rather scared. We had to traverse across a really narrow rockface – I'm not convinced that we shouldn't have been roped up, but I was assured that it would be fine – and it was only about 30 ft that looked scary. I was petrified, but Jack gave me a little pep talk. He also handed me some glucose tablets and suggested I eat a few of them. Surprisingly they really help. I guess a hit of sugar helps you to focus on the task at hand, and I took a deep breath and started traversing across the rock, leaning into the rock as much as possible as Jack had advised. At the other end I grabbed Declan's hand and he helped me up the last few feet.

"Well done Lily, we went a little off course there. I didn't mean us to come up that part. I was a little worried how you would cope with that but you obviously are made of strong stuff," declared Declan.

I felt very proud of myself. It was a similar feeling to crossing the finish line at parkrun. I guess it's the endorphins starting to flow. I knew that I had Jack to thank for giving me advice, instilling me with confidence and willing me on. He was also right behind me at all times, so I felt well looked after.

We stopped again for a quick lunch. This time I wasn't really hungry as it was probably only an hour ago that we ate last. But I'm always happy to eat and at least I knew that I was burning off the calories this time. We polished off the rest of the sandwiches and had a can of diet coke each. Again we were able to enjoy the exquisite views and relax for a short time.

I asked what the afternoon adventures entailed and learnt that actually it was pretty much downhill most of the rest of the way. I was pretty tired – my legs were aching, my arms were aching, I had a bunch of scratches & bruises so I wasn't too displeased that the afternoon would be significantly easier than the morning. Jack warned me not to get complacent however – it's very easy to get hurt scrambling downwards if you are not careful.

We set off again and completed the final few, downhill kilometres at a steady pace. There was no need to race and we got to enjoy the spectacular scenery. Although going downhill sounded easy, my legs were killing me. My quads felt absolutely shot and were rather jelly like. When we were nearing the lower slopes the terrain flattened out and Jack grabbed hold of my hand and I nestled into his side. I felt so comfortable and happy with him. There was never any awkward moments and no difficult silences. The conversation flowed, we laughed and we joked.

It really did feel like the perfect day. After the emotional rollercoaster that I'd been on for the last couple of weeks, it felt fabulous to feel settled and happy. Jack was so handsome, fun, bright, caring, patient, chilled out and just fantastic company.

When we made it back to the campsite we gathered up some firewood before collapsing onto the floor. I couldn't believe that I was hungry yet again. The boys started a fire leaving Annie & I to sort out the food. We had sausages and pasta to make. Out came the little frying pan and a little saucepan to boil the pasta. It was very simple but totally delicious.

We had a few more cans of beer & cider left so each settled down with a drink. Declan had brought a portable radio so we listened to Radio 1's Saturday night tunes. It really was the perfect end to the perfect day. As I sat there, snuggled up to Jack, I suddenly realised that I hadn't thought of James or Rob even once during the whole day. That spoke volumes to me, and I realised that it was good that I had left Rob, and I was more caught up on the 'idea' of the relationship with James than James as a person. I guess I really didn't know him that well – I think I was more excited about being able to double-date with Molly than anything else.

Jack asked what I was thinking, so I outlined my thoughts. Jack thought Molly sounded cool, and said that he was looking forward to meeting her. It was probably the first time I had really thought much further forward than this weekend, and I realised that I was really looking forward to introducing Jack to my friends and family.

I liked the idea that I didn't meet Jack in a pub or club. It was nice that we'd met doing something that we had in common. I really liked the idea that he was fit and enjoyed outdoor activities. Like any normal young person, of course I liked nights out and hanging out with friends –

but actually I really enjoyed doing activities more. I was hopeful that in the next few years I would experience all sorts of new adventures – I wanted to fly a glider, go bungy jumping, go parasailing, lie on an exotic beach, swim in beautiful turquoise waters and learn to scuba dive. There were so many adventures to be had – and it was lovely to feel like I had met someone that was interested in similar things.

When I'm old, grey and immobile, I want to be able to look back on my life and smile at the activities, scrapes and experiences that I go through. Life is an adventure, and I was really excited that I might just have found someone who had a similar outlook to me. Of course, it's very early days, and I don't want to get my hopes up too much, but I really had had the most awesome day.

As I lay kissing Jack that night, wrapped up in our respective sleeping bags and secure in our tent, I had a smile on my face and butterflies in my stomach. What a lucky girl I was.

Chapter 18

Once again we were up bright and early after a good night's sleep. It was another beautiful morning with sunshine and a light breeze. We had been really blessed with the weather in recent weeks. Jack & I bounced out of bed pretty quickly as it was our turn to cook breakfast. Breakfast this morning consisted of sausages & fried eggs with some very slightly stale bread rolls. It still tasted great though.

We were all due back at work on Monday morning, so we decided we had better do a short scramble/walk/climb this morning and be homeward bound by lunchtime. We had pretty much run out of food now so decided we would stop and eat at some point on the way home.

Declan and Jack decided that we should tackle Y Gribin Ridge which is a fairly short but extremely beautiful scramble. Normally, people proceed straight onto Lliwedd but due to our having only a few hours, we did an out and back route. Today there was nothing to scare me. After the adventures of yesterday I felt confident & relaxed. My legs were certainly aching but I felt very happy. I didn't even need too much of Jack's assistance today. We spent more time laughing & talking than we did discussing the actual route & scrambling technique.

The rest of the day flew by and by 4pm we were half way home and I could feel my eyes starting to close. It had been a fabulous but tiring weekend. It had been so nice to switch off and concentrate on the walking and the fun times, and not worry about any of the recent events. Molly texted me as we were nearing home and I arranged to meet up with her on Tuesday night for a catch up. It seemed like we hadn't seen each other for ages but I was far too tired to contemplate venturing out tonight.

By Tuesday evening I was really excited to meet up with Molly. I turned up ten minutes early in the pub and for once made it to the bar before Molly. It was a nice change for me to have our drinks waiting on the table.

"You look amazing," exclaimed Molly as she walked in, gave me a hug and sat down.

"Thanks – so do you. You are positively glowing." I replied. Molly did actually look stunning – she was tanned, and had the biggest smile on her face.

"So what's happening Mols?" I asked.

Molly filled me in on her last couple of weekends. She had had a weekend away with Harry a couple of weeks back and spent most of this weekend hanging out with him too. They were very firmly coupled up and she looked absolutely delighted. I was so happy for her.

I was pleased to feel that I was actually more keen to tell her about my weekend away with Jack, then I was to ask about James. It seemed I had moved on more easily than I thought I would. Of course, it helps having a drop dead gorgeous, sexy, fun, amazing man to move on with.

Molly was pretty horrified to hear about the scrambling routes around Snowdonia – almost as much as she was to hear about camping in a tent. Both of those ideas were pretty unpleasant to her and she just couldn't get her head around why I was so happy about them. It really was surprising why we were such close friends when we were quite so different.

Molly's weekend away with Harry had consisted of staying in a nice hotel, having a five-course meal in a posh restaurant and walking around the harbour of a little coastal village in Norfolk. Whilst that sounds fun, I think my weekend with Jack was more memorable & more fun.

"So when do I get to meet the infamous Jack?" asked Molly.

"He's hardly infamous," I laughed. "He's just drop dead gorgeous, funny, laid back, caring, patient, kind and extremely sexy".

Molly laughed. She was really happy for me too. We both sat sipping on our drinks with the biggest smiles on our faces. We decided that we would have to arrange a double-date for this weekend – if Harry & Jack were up for that. I said that Jack had already mentioned that he'd like to meet Molly, and Molly was sure that Harry would be keen to meet up too.

Towards the end of the evening Molly asked if I wanted an update on James? To be honest, I had actually forgotten about him for a few days, and I wasn't sure if I did want to hear about him. But now that she had mentioned his name my curiosity would need to be satisfied.

"Go on then, how is James doing?" I asked.

"Well, the first weekend they spent together James & Jasmine were really happy to be back together again. They had seen each other last week a few times and everything seemed to be progressing well. But then this weekend Harry happened to mention to James that you had gone away for a weekend with Jack, and James demanded to know who Jack was. He appeared quite jealous and almost ignored Jasmine whilst talking with Harry. Jasmine had sat quietly and just watched while James continued to question Harry about the two of you. James soon realised that he had made a bit of a 'faux-pas' and quickly changed the subject and included Jasmine in the conversation. The damage was done though. There was a definite tension for the rest of the day between them and we got the feeling that words would be had once they left".

I sipped on my cider contemplating what Molly had said. I wasn't really sure how I felt. I certainly didn't feel too bothered about James & Jasmine. I think I had accepted the situation and started to move on, so I wasn't sure that I really needed to hear what Molly had told me. I felt more excited about Jack then I had done about James. I explained this to Molly and she seemed pleased to hear that I wasn't upset in any way. The conversation moved on to more trivial things and Molly shortly had me in absolute stitches recounting a story that Evie had told her about some boy that she had pulled last weekend. He'd got that drunk that he'd lost his wallet, lost his watch, lost his phone and totally forgot her name in the morning. She'd said it was lucky that he was so cute or she would have been rather unimpressed by that behaviour. And luckily he made a mean fry up to redeem himself.

After making loose arrangements for Friday night (subject to the boys approval of course) we bid each other goodbye and headed home.

Friday night rolled around and we arranged to meet up at the new-ish cocktail bar. Molly & I got ready together and met up with Jack & Harry at the bar. I was really excited for Jack to meet with Molly, and felt pretty confident that they would get on well. I wasn't so sure about Harry as he was best friends with James of course.

Once we arrived Jack offered to get the first round in. So, whilst he wandered off to the bar Molly blurted out....

"Well, he's pretty hot isn't he."

"Thanks then," huffed Harry.

"Not as hot as you of course, Harry. But he is a good looking guy," countered Molly quickly.

"Well recovered," smirked Harry.

I burst out laughing at their exchange. And luckily they both joined in. I was pleased that Molly liked the look of Jack.

Jack soon arrived back with the drinks and distributed them accordingly. Molly immediately started quizzing Jack, hardly giving him a chance for a breath.

Jack explained (for Harry's benefit mainly) how we had met at parkrun, and outlined our hiking/climbing weekend. By the time half an hour had passed we were all chatting and laughing together. The very slight hostility between the boys had more than disappeared and it seemed like they would make good friends.

I had taken a bit of a backseat during this chatting – unusual for me. But it was lovely just to listen to my best mate, Jack & Harry all getting to know each other.

"So, what's your plans this weekend Jack?" asked Harry.

"Well, I can't tell you that," Jack replied. "It's a secret."

"What do you mean?" asked Harry.

"I have a surprise for Lily tomorrow, but I haven't told her yet".

That sounded exciting. We hadn't actually got as far as discussing the weekend yet. I had been hoping we could see each other, but as it's still early days I didn't want to seem too keen.

"Ooooh, that sounds good," I said. "What's the surprise?"

Unfortunately Jack wouldn't expand on the surprise. He just told me to wear trousers and be ready at 9am. That meant we would miss parkrun, but apparently it would be worth it. I was really excited. So far, all the times that I had been with Jack had been great fun. He hadn't put a foot wrong and I was loving getting to know him more.

As we left the bar, Jack offered to walk me home to which I readily agreed. We had had a lovely evening, and it had been fun yet relaxed. On the walk home I bugged Jack a little to try and find out the surprise, but he wouldn't give me any hints. I couldn't wait for the next day.

As Jack dropped me off at the door, we had the most amazing kiss. It brought butterflies to my stomach and I felt this deep joy & excitement. I invited him in, but he declined as Mum appeared to have already gone to bed and he didn't want to disturb her. He's really thoughtful as well as gorgeous.

Chapter 19

I drifted off to sleep with a big smile on my face. I had a truly wonderful dream about Jack and woke up with my heart beating wildly, all hot and sweaty. I relaxed into my pillow and dozed off some more, still thinking about Jack. I couldn't wait to see him.

Jack arrived on the dot of 9am. As I walked out he opened the car door for me. It's nice that he is so thoughtful and makes really nice gestures like that – he's a proper gentlemen.

We drove for about 30 minutes out into some really rural, beautiful countryside. We then turned into a drive which had a sign on the outside saying 'Lofthouse Stables'. I turned to Jack and asked if we were going riding? On horses? He said yes, and I couldn't wait.

Despite being an outgoing and adventurous kind of girl, I actually had never ridden a horse. Jack & I had had this discussion last weekend so he was aware of this. The only time I had done anything similar was a donkey-ride on Weston-Super-Mare beach when I was a kid. But I don't think that really counts.

"So can you ride Jack?" I asked.

"A little," he replied.

As we pulled into the car park, we excitedly jumped out of the car. We made our way into the courtyard of stables and headed to the office.

"Hello Jack," said the middle-aged lady carrying a saddle.

"Hi Aunt Mags," replied Jack.

"Ummm, hold on a minute," I exclaimed to Jack. "This is your aunt. Does this mean you ride a lot?"

"I certainly don't ride a lot," said Jack, "but over the years I guess I have ridden on an occasional basis. I can hold my own at least".

Now I was starting to feel nervous. Knowing Jack as I did, I was pretty confident he would be a fairly decent rider. And I would look like a complete idiot.

Aunt Mags was introduced to me (as Maggie) and we shook hands. She was a really lovely, bubbly and welcoming lady so I felt quite comfortable.

"We've got Paddy ready for you Jack, and we have a lovely old mare for you to ride Lily, called Rosie. She is a real sweetheart to ride and will look after you well. She's over 30 years old."

That sounded pretty old to me, so I felt quite comfortable. Rosie was brought out for me. She was already tacked up (wearing a saddle & bridle) by one of the stable girls and she immediately started nudging me for a polo. Maggie handed me a packet and I gave Rosie a couple of them. At least we were friends from the start. Rosie was apparently about 15.2hh and was a chestnut mare. She looked massive to me, but apparently wasn't that big.

Then Jack went to collect Paddy. As he returned leading this massive, beautiful, amazing looking black beauty, my heart missed a few beats. He was a stunning horse, and Jack looked totally confident handling him.

I led Rosie over to the mounting block and Aunt Mags explained how I should get on. Once on board she explained how to hold the reins and the basics that I needed to know. A squeeze of the legs to move forwards, the reins for left and right. I was warned not to lean forwards as that

106

encouraged the horse to go faster. I was reassured that Rosie was a perfect horse to learn on. She wasn't lazy, but would look after me well. She had never been known to buck, rear or behave badly.

We headed over into a very large outdoor arena. The surface looked like sand & rubber – so at least it would be soft if I fell off. To start with we just walked around the edge while I got used to the motion. Rosie was an absolutely angel and did exactly what I asked her to do. She was calm and obedient, but walked forwards nicely and confidently. I was told to sit up, to keep my heels down and my elbows in by my side. After a few minutes I started turning left, right and riding some circles as directed by Maggie. I had a big grin on my face and really enjoyed myself. Maggie told me that I was a natural, and I enjoyed the praise. I was really pleased at how well I had seemed to get on – although I think I did have the perfect horse.

Maggie asked if I wanted to try a trot. Which of course I did. She told me to hold on to the front of the saddle (which is apparently called the pommel) so I gave Rosie a squeeze with my legs and on she trotted.

Oh my. I was jiggling about all over the place, although things improved when I realised I had let go of the pommel. I was glad that I had put a sports bra on. After a minute or so Maggie explained about rising trot and encouraged me to give it a go. Well, I was hardly an expert, but I did manage to string together a few 'up-downs' in a row and when I managed that I actually felt vaguely like I could ride a little. Of course, then I missed the timing, and totally bumped all over the place. Each time I lost my balance Rosie kindly came back to the walk so I could get myself collected up again. After about 10 minutes of attempting a number of rising trots I managed to complete an entire circuit of the arena before losing the rhythm. However, I was exhausted, so had a walk for a rest.

It was Jack's turn. So far, Jack had just been walking around the arena on the beautiful Paddy. He soon proceeded to a trot and looked wonderful doing circles and different shapes in this lovely, constant rhythm.

He moved up a gear into a beautiful canter. It looked effortless, he looked totally in control and like something out of a Jilly Cooper novel. Jack and Paddy moved as one. So much for 'I can hold my own'. He truly looked like a professional.

Maggie shouted out to Jack that Paddy could do with a quick jump, so Jack headed towards a cross pole situated in the middle of the school. They jumped the fence as one, in a beautiful, rhythmical motion. He then turned up the school towards a small spread fence, which they popped over in style.

He sat up after the next corner and appeared to gather Paddy together to make him a little more bouncy, and he jumped what looked like a gate. Again it was like an amazing fluid motion – no bumps or unbalancing happening here. It was amazing to watch and I was thoroughly enjoying myself – having almost forgotten that I myself was still walking around on the lovely Rosie.

"Go on then Jack," shouted Maggie. "Over the triple bar".

I looked around and saw this massive spread fence which I guessed must be the triple bar as it consisted of 3 coloured poles. It must have been over 4 foot high and about 7 foot wide. Surely not? Jack wasn't going to jump that was he? Jack grinned at me as he cantered past on the corner and then Paddy's stride started to lengthen as he approached the huge jump.

As Paddy got closer to the fence, I could see that he seemed to be locked onto the fence by the expression in his eyes and his ears which were pushed totally forward. He was totally focussed and I could see the muscles tensing and gleaming in his hindquarters. He thundered towards the spread and then jumped an amazing arc over the fence. As they flew through the air Jack let out a 'whoop' which seemed to startle Paddy.

As Paddy landed over the fence, he seemed to quicken in pace. His ears went back and he suddenly did a massive buck and Jack flew through the air and landed about 20 feet away onto the sand/rubber surface. My heart missed a beat or two as I suddenly worried that Jack would be seriously injured. But he jumped straight back on his feet and laughed. Paddy was careering around the arena leaping and bucking. I was not sure what was best for me to do, but Paddy soon stopped and settled back down. He came towards Rosie and stood beside us. I leaned down and reached for his reins to hold him.

"Sorry Paddy boy," said Jack as he took the reins off of me and gave the horse a pat. He grinned up and assured me that he was fine. No harm done other than a slightly bruised ego. It was a relief that horse and rider were fine.

Maggie was now with us and had a quick look around the horse but was happy that there was no damage to the horse, rider or tack (apparently a collective term for the saddle, bridle and other bits and pieces on the horse). Jack apologised to Maggie and admitted that there was just a small chance that he might have been showing off a little.

Maggie didn't mind and just laughed at him. At least the horse had had a good exercise.

We walked the horses around for a few more minutes to cool them down – well, to cool Paddy down. Rosie had not even broken a sweat with her just walking and trotting. But I was really pleased for my first ever horse-ride. Maggie reassured me that I had done really well, and suggested we come back again soon. Jack & I both assured her that we would do exactly that.

We put the horses away, and one of the stable-girls showed me how to 'untack' Rosie so that she could go back in her stable and eat hay. She would apparently go out on a hack this afternoon which is where you ride around fields & tracks. Maybe we would have a go at that next time – I would like to try it.

Chapter 20

"So what did you think of your surprise, Lily?" enquired Jack.

"Oh my goodness, it was awesome." I answered. "That was truly magical. Rosie was such a sweetheart that I didn't even feel scared – aside from when I thought you had injured yourself."

Jack laughed. "It was totally my fault – I was showing off. I startled the fabulous Paddy by whooping so loudly after the jump".

"I'm just happy there was no damage to you or the horse. But thank you so much for arranging it. I'm really grateful" I said.

We discussed what we wanted to do next. It was still only Saturday lunchtime, and we were both starving so we decided we'd treat ourselves to a pub lunch on the way home. Jack knew of a reputable pub just a couple of miles out of our way, so we went there.

The Ghostly Goat was a big old-fashioned pub. The car park was full and we could see that the gardens were full of tables as well as the restaurant. We weren't sure if we'd be able to find a table, but luckily a couple vacated one just as we were walking through the garden. Jack settled down at the table and I headed to the bar for a couple of drinks and some menus. Jack had a lager shandy (as he was driving) and I had a pint of cider.

I headed back to the table carrying the menus and the two drinks, and was focused on trying not to spill them. Just as I reached the table, I heard a voice that I recognised. Sat with his back to us a few tables away was James. Opposite him was a strikingly pretty girl who had a very ugly scowl on her face. I guessed that this was Jasmine. I could see that in happier times she would be incredibly pretty, but right now she looked extremely grumpy. I could hear James reasoning with her in a low, steady voice.

"Are you ok, Lily? You've gone very pale" asked Jack.

OMG….. I'd forgotten where I was for a moment there. I tore my glance off of James's back and gently put the drinks on the table. I smiled at Jack and apologised.

"Sorry, sorry. I didn't mean to be rude. I just had a bit of a shock" I explained.

I pointed out James and Jasmine to Jack and he was very understanding of the situation.

"Do you want to get out of here and go somewhere else?" he offered.

"Um, no need. I think they are leaving anyway" I replied as I could see out of the corner of my eye that Jasmine and James had stood up.

They started to walk towards us, winding through the tables until they got near us when James suddenly stopped. He had spotted me. Jasmine was following him and almost walked into his back as he had stopped that abruptly.

"Lily," said James. "I wasn't expecting to see you here?"

"Likewise" I replied. "I've never been here before. This is my friend Jack. Jack – this is James".

The boys murmured a hello to each other, then James turned and indicated the girl.

"This is Jasmine. Jasmine – this is Lily & Jack".

"Pleased to meet you" said Jasmine. Although she scowled and looked like she had been slapped in the face. "We are leaving – come on James" she insisted.

"Um goodbye Lily. Look after yourself" murmured James as he followed Jasmine out of the garden.

"Well that wasn't awkward at all" offered Jack. He looked rather unsettled.

We both took a sip of our drinks and then started to chat some more about the morning's adventure. After a few minutes talking we both relaxed again, and got back into the easy comfortable way that we had with each other.

We then proceeded to enjoy a leisurely lunch. We both chose the pub special – a homemade Steak & Ale pie with chips and salad. It was truly delicious and very filling. We topped it off with another drink each and then shared a chocolate brownie between us. We were too full to have a dessert each, but it was really good to share one.

Jack dropped me off after lunch as I had promised Mum that I'd go with her to a nearby town for some shopping. We hadn't had a Mum/daughter day for a long time, so it was well overdue. Jack also told me that he was working away this week, so I wouldn't get to see him. In fact, he was working up in Scotland, so would be leaving Sunday morning. I was quite gutted. I did feel like I was falling for him very quickly. Maybe it wasn't such a bad thing that he wasn't around this week so we had a little more space from each other.

Chapter 21

I'd arranged to meet up with Molly tonight after spending the afternoon with Mum. I felt like we hadn't really had much time just the two of us, and Harry was off with some friends planning a stag do, so Molly was at a loose end too.

We arranged to go to the pub most local to Molly. We didn't go there very often, but it was a decent enough pub. Particularly useful as it was quite cheap. As I arrived, Molly was already sitting at a table with a pint of cider for me and what looked like a gin & tonic for herself. As soon as I sat down, she put her phone away which she had been messaging away on.

After some initial chit chat, Molly asked me how things were going. Had I heard from James and how were things going with Jack?

"We had the best morning today. He took me to his Aunt's riding stables. We had a lesson on horses. I was so excited. I rode this beautiful chestnut mare called Rosie, and Jack rode this beautiful big, black horse called Paddy. It was pretty steady for me – I just walked and trotted. But Jack was cantering and even did some jumping. He looked really good until he got a bit overexcited and scared Paddy who then bucked him off. Luckily he was ok other than dented pride".

"Oh my god", said Molly. "That sounds absolutely amazing. I'm so jealous. I used to ride for a couple of years when I was a kid but I don't think I've sat on a horse since I was about 7. How are you feeling now? Are your legs aching?"

114

"Too right they are," I laughed. "I feel like John Wayne. I can hardly walk. My legs are really sore. It was well worth it though. I absolutely loved it".

"It was lucky that Jack wasn't hurt," remarked Molly. "He could have done himself some proper damage."

"He really could," I agreed. "He proper flew through the air, but luckily it was a soft surface to land on, and he got straight back up again. I think he was showing off a little bit, but up until that point I was incredibly impressed as he did look like a really competent rider."

I then brought Molly up to speed on the pub lunch after and bumping into James and Jasmine.

"That's a bit of a coincidence bumping into them like that," said Molly. "How did you feel when you saw him?"

"I felt shocked initially because I was not expecting to see them. But Jasmine looked like she had eaten a wasp. She was definitely not happy. In fact, she looked downright stroppy. And that seemed to get worse once she had been introduced to us."

"Do you think you will hear from him again?" asked Molly.

"I don't know. He will have certainly got the message that I've moved on too now, so there is no need for him to have any contact with me really. However, as you and Harry are dating, he might think it's important for us to stay friends as we are likely to see them every now and again. And on that note, how are things going for you two?" I asked.

"Things were going great," said Molly. "But the last week or so Harry hasn't seemed quite as keen as he was. It's almost like he's gradually moving away from spending time with me. Like tonight......he says he's meeting friends to plan a stag night…..but I have no idea if he's making an excuse up to not see me. I do feel like that might be the case but I don't really know".

"You were staying at his most nights weren't you?" I asked.

"Well I was," replied Molly, "but then last week he was working away, and this week he says he's working away again. But I'm sure I saw him Thursday night driving in his car the opposite direction to me, but he says he didn't get back until Friday. I'm a bit confused to be honest. I definitely feel that he's not giving me the attention that he was. But equally, I don't want to sound suspicious or like I'm being needy as that never works either".

We continued chatting about Molly's relationship, but we just started going round in circles. It seemed that there was nothing wrong particularly, no bad words, no argument, nothing specific. Molly just felt that he was cooling off and distancing himself a bit. I guess that time will tell eventually.

"So," said Molly. "Going back to James. I fear that all is not well in the James & Jasmine camp."

"Really?" I exclaimed. "They've only been back together a week or so."

"Well, that might be right" responded Molly. "But Jasmine is not happy about the fact that James was dating you. She's giving him a really hard time about it. And it's not going down that well with James at all".

"It is a difficult situation, because he had no idea that she was coming back again. She did kind of spring it on James and it was just bad luck that we had just got together. I think if we'd been together longer, he would

116

have had more loyalty to me, but it was such early days. We hadn't even had a conversation about if we were exclusively dating, although, I think we were. Well, it seemed that way to me anyway".

"Definitely," agreed Molly. "You might not have been official, but you both were quite into each other and everything had been going well. Then of course Jasmine had to turn up to spoil things. Still, it might be interesting to see what happens in due course. And it gives you a backup plan to Jack.".

"Molly, that's outrageous. I don't need a backup plan. You make me sound awful. I would be quite happy being on my own. I don't need a man. And I certainly only want one if they add value to my life."

"Well, I'd say you are doing quite well then," laughed Molly. "You seem to have had a lot of fun with both James and Jack".

"To be fair, as much as I know them, they are quite similar in character. They are both outgoing, fun, confident, sporty and they both seem kind, caring and considerate as well. I guess I'm lucky to be in this situation really – I was lucky enough to meet Jack just as James decided that he was going to try and resurrect his relationship with Jasmine. I couldn't have asked for better timing.

We chatted for a few more minutes and decided that the next few weeks should be interesting. We'd see where things go with Molly & Harry. Were they the real deal or was it just exciting for the initial few weeks? Then we'd see how things worked out with James & Jasmine and myself and Jack. On that note, we finished up our drinks and headed home.

Chapter 22

I woke up Sunday morning to a warm, clear, sunny day. It was nice to wake up without a hangover and I didn't even feel tired. Today was unusual in that I didn't have any plans. Jack was away for work this morning so I wouldn't see him. Molly was out for the day with her sister. What to do?

In view of the fact that I needed to get some more running miles in, I pulled on my trainers and headed out the door. I thought I would aim to do 10km. In fact, to make it mentally a bit easier, I aimed to run to where parkrun is held, run around the parkrun course, run an extra loop along the bluebell route that Jack previously showed me, then run home. That would equate to approximately 10km and hopefully would mean that it didn't feel too long. It would be the longest run I had done in a very long time.

Twenty minutes later I was on the parkrun course. Running it alone seems quite bizarre when you are used to running it with so many other people. As I head towards the bridge I see a familiar face running the other way. It looks like James. As we get closer I see that it is in fact James. We smile at each other and he gives me a quick wave. As I get level with him he turns around and starts jogging next to me, asking if I mind if he joins me for a bit.

"That would be nice," I state. "I'd be glad of the company as I'm attempting my first 10km."

"That's great," says James. "Good for you. I'm impressed".

"I haven't done it yet," I laugh.

"I'm glad I bumped into you," replied James. "I was hoping that I might. I'd really like to talk to you."

"Go ahead," I say. "I'm listening".

"I miss you," says James. "I miss spending time with you, and I miss the laughs that we had".

"What about Jasmine?" I ask.

"It's not what I expected," replied James. "She's really changed. I thought I would feel the same as before she went away, but I don't at all. She used to be really happy, good fun, relaxed & sociable. Now she seems clingy, needy and desperately insecure. I'm not sure what happened to her in the US but I did think it was a bit odd that she came back so quickly. I don't think it's going to work out."

"I'm sorry to hear that," I said truthfully. I wasn't even lying. I was sorry. Whilst I did like James a lot I had totally understood the situation and he had handled it like a gentlemen and been respectful to me. And, I feel like I've moved on. I've had fun with Jack and I guess that had stopped me missing James.

However, I did feel really relaxed and comfortable running next to him. From the moment I met him we had always got along well and enjoyed each other's company.

"So are you and Jasmine still together?" I ask.

"Well, yes, currently. But I have discussed my feelings with her and she knows that things aren't going well. But, whatever happens, I really do care for her and I want her to be happy. She needs to open up and talk to me and I just get the impression that there is a story to tell and she's not telling it to me. I want to help her and I want to be there for her. I'm just not sure that that should be in a boyfriend capacity. Maybe we'd be better off as friends," explains James.

"Well, she probably wouldn't be very happy that we are running together," I stated.

"True," countered James. "But, it's not like we planned to meet. We literally just bumped into each other. What's going on with you anyway? I take it that the Jack guy that you introduced me to is a new boyfriend? I think I recognise him. Doesn't he go to parkrun sometimes?"

"Yes, that's right. I met him at parkrun and we got chatting from there. We've been seeing each other a short time, but he's really nice. Good fun. No baggage. No exes cropping up." I say pointedly.

"OK, OK, give me a break," replied James. "I had no idea Jasmine was going to come back. It was a total surprise".

By this point we were back at the bridge and it was time for me to head off back towards home. The time had flown by whilst I was running with James, and a quick check of my watch told me that I had run 8km already. I actually felt fine, and no worse than running 5km. Hopefully that's a good sign that my stamina is starting to build up. I said goodbye to James and headed off towards home.

Once on my own my pace slowed considerably. It's surprising how much difference it makes running with someone for motivation. Maybe my brain thinking so much was slowing me down. I could almost feel my brain cogs whirring, thinking about James and Jasmine, and then thinking about Jack.

The last kilometre home started to hurt. It's amazing how you can be swinging along thinking that you feel pretty good, then suddenly it's like you run into a

120

swamp. Your legs get heavy, the fatigue sets in and you just feel drained. I hit the 10km mark a street before my house which is ideal as it gives me a chance to power walk. I can loosen up my running muscles and do a few stretches on the way back home. It gives me a chance to get my heart rate back to near-normal before I stop. This is much better on the body than just suddenly stopping dead and collapsing into a chair.

As I let myself into the house my Mum steps out of the lounge clapping.

"What are you clapping for?" I ask.

"That's your longest run in years Lily. I'm really proud of you," Mum states.

It actually made tears well up in my eyes. Bizarrely, I do find I can get a bit emotional after a good run. I might end up crying if I eventually make the finish line of the half marathon later this year.

I head upstairs immediately for a hot shower and a bit of a lie down on my bed to recover. That was tough, but I feel good, if a little tired. And the conversation with James has given me food for thought.

Chapter 23

The week passed uneventfully. Jack was away with work, so I didn't see him at all. He did message most mornings and evenings though which was nice. Thursday night Molly popped in on her way home from work. She asked what plans I had for the weekend, and I said that I didn't have any at this point. We were sat in the back garden, and it was another lovely evening. It wasn't hot enough yet that we were being bothered by too many insects. But warm enough that we could sit outside without a jumper on.

I brought her up to speed with my conversation with James at the weekend. She asked how I was feeling and I said that I was trying not to think too much about it. I was happy with how things were going with Jack and I had no desire to get involved with James while Jasmine was still on the radar.

"What would you do if Jasmine & James split up?" asked Molly.

"Well, not much at the moment," I replied. "I certainly wouldn't go running back to him straight away. I did like him, but I don't like to feel second best. And things are going well with Jack so I'd like to see where that goes really."

"That's totally understandable," agreed Molly.

"How are things with you and Harry?" I asked.

"Well, he's working away this week but he's been a lot more communicative and we are making plans to spend time together at the weekend. I think maybe he was just busy with work, and I was used to him being around. I confused that with thinking he was distancing himself from me. On reflection, I think I was wrong," replied Molly. "I'm not really used to being needy but I've not felt like this about someone in a long time. I was single for quite some time, and I've really enjoyed having a boyfriend again."

I gave Molly a hug. It was nice to see her excited about someone. She really did seem happy with Harry so I hoped it worked out for them both.

"I wouldn't be upset if you did get back with James again," stated Molly. "It was fun when the four of us were going on double dates".

"It was," I laughed. "But that's really not a reason to date him. I want to be someone's number one. And I clearly wasn't that for James".

"I'm not convinced about that," countered Molly. "I think he was confused and felt like he owed it to Jasmine and their history to give their relationship another go. But it's clearly not working. They don't have that same camaraderie that you two had. Jasmine never looks happy. She's very highly strung and looks miserable all of the time. And James seems to go quite quiet when he's with her. It's really not much fun spending time with the two of them. It's quite a painful experience to be honest."

We continued to chat together. I didn't want to make plans for the weekend yet as I wasn't sure what was happening with Jack. But we did arrange to meet up Sunday night if we hadn't got together before then. Molly and Harry were busy Friday night (just the two of them) but she was keen to meet up Saturday night if I was able.

I had a quiet Friday night in as Jack wasn't going to get back home until around midnight. I was also planning on going to parkrun so was happy with that. I decided tomorrow would be a good day to have another crack at my PB. I'd managed another interval session during the week and I was certainly starting to feel a little stronger and like I had a bit more stamina.

Saturday morning was another dry and sunny start. It was due to rain later but not until about midday. I power walked to the park which I thought would be a good warm up for me without wasting too much energy. As soon as I got to the start area, James strolled up to me with a big, beaming smile.

"I wondered if you would be here. You are looking good today," James said.

"Thanks," I replied. "I'm feeling pretty good. Going to have a crack at a new PB today."

"Again? Would you like me to pace you?" asked James.

"No thanks," I replied. "I'm good to run on my own".

At that, I spied a familiar figure out of the corner of my eye. It was Jack. He walked towards me with a big smile which wavered slightly when he saw who I was talking to. The boys shook each other's hand as they said hi to each other. Jack then gave me a hug making James look a little embarrassed.

"Well, it was good to bump into you, Lily," said James. "I'll leave you to it. Have a good run. I hope you get your PB".

I said thanks and turned to Jack as James melted away into the crowds of other parkrunners.

"I hope I wasn't disturbing anything," said Jack.

"Not at all," I replied. "I had no idea he would be here. I'm glad you are though. I've missed you". And I had. It felt good to give Jack another hug. I loved the feel of his strong arms around me.

"So, it's PB today is it?" asked Jack.

"I hope so," I replied. "But I may be expecting a little too much. I was amazingly pleased with my last PB and I feel it will be hard to beat it."

At that, the Run Director started the briefing. It was a very vibrant lady who was RD this week. So we turned to the front and listened to what was being said. We then headed to the start area.

3-2-1 parkrun. Said the RD. And a ring of the starting bell accompanied her.

Off we set. We were nearer the front than the back, and within about 5 seconds we were running at a pretty good pace. I was slightly concerned I might not be able to keep this going and indeed, when I looked at my watch we were going about 30 seconds/mile too fast. I slowed slightly and allowed a bunch of faster people to overtake me. I then seemed to be in around the right place for my pace as the field started to string out along the course and no-one else was overtaking me. It's always quite hard to figure out where you need to start from unless you know the other runners well.

I was aiming for a sub-28 minute run. Which would be an amazing achievement if I pulled it off. But I had been doing two or three runs a week including a longer run (by my standards) and some intervals. It definitely seemed to be working as I could feel myself getting stronger and able to hold a little more pace. I actually was starting to feel like I had earned the 'runner' label. Rather than just being someone that runs a little bit.

At the half-way point I was starting to think that maybe sub-28 minutes was aiming too high. I was struggling. My legs were starting to feel heavy and my lungs were starting to burn. Bizarrely though, for the first time, I didn't hate the feeling. I was starting to appreciate the fittening process and enjoying the benefits. I eased off for about 10 seconds and let my pace drop, then heard Jack behind me encouraging me on. I hadn't realised he was there. I had lost him in the busyness of the start and had assumed that he had gone ahead. Clearly, he was supporting me. This made me feel happy, and it gave me a little extra energy. I managed to pick up the pace back to what I had been running previously.

Jack then came up beside me and told me that I was doing a great job. I gasped back that I couldn't talk, and he told me not to try. He told me to just focus on keeping my arms going at the same pace as that would keep my legs going automatically. I hadn't really thought of that before, but he was right. Somehow, mentally, it's easier to make your arms go faster, and your legs just seem to go along for the ride. The psychology and physiology of running is truly fascinating.

We were now approaching the last kilometre of the run. The first half is on the flat, and then the second half is slightly downhill towards the finish funnel. Jack advised me to just keep the same pace on the flat and then use the hill to quicken slightly to the finish funnel. I didn't think I had anything left in the tank, but with his encouragement and the help of the downhill stretch, I was able to get my arms and legs turning over a little quicker. The 'pace' of a run is determined by the cadence of the stride and the length of the stride. The downhill stretch enabled me to increase both my cadence and my length of stride. I felt like I was sprinting – I envisaged being at the end of an Olympic race, and people cheering me towards the line. That is until a little kid, only about 8 years old, went past me like I was stopped dead.

I smiled to myself and headed towards the finish funnel. Over the line, stop the watch, try not to collapse and hold out my hand for a finish token. Once again I struggled to breathe. I needed to lie down. My legs felt wobbly.

As I exited the finish funnel, Jack grabbed hold of my arm and led me over towards a clear patch of grass. There were loads of parkrunners milling around and I needed space to recover. I bent nearly double and started trying to catch my breath. I was almost hyperventilating. I don't think I had ever put that much effort into a run.

Jack had put his arm around me and lowered me to the floor. I lay on my back looking at him silhouetted against the sky. I felt truly lucky. He is such a good guy, as well as handsome, charming and fun. My breathing had recovered now so I sat up and Jack sat beside me.

"That was awesome. You were awesome. Do you know what time you finished in?" Jack asked.

"No idea. I was far too exhausted to look at my watch," I laughed.

"You finished in just over 26 minutes." exclaimed Jack.

"What?" I stared incredulously at Jack. "Are you serious? That's amazing. I never, ever expected to do that.

"It is pretty amazing considering only a few weeks ago you were running parkrun in over 30 minutes. You should be well proud of yourself" said Jack.

"I am, I am," I almost cried with happiness. "That was so hard but it also felt pretty amazing too. I really put 100% of effort into that run. I'm not sure I'll ever be able to do it again."

"Well, I think your finish time was around 26:12 give or take a few seconds," replied Jack. "That is brilliant. I'm so happy for you and so proud of you".

"Well, you've helped me," I countered. "You've helped me make running a part of my lifestyle and we've talked about doing longer runs to increase my stamina, and intervals to increase my speed. I'm just putting into practice what we've discussed. I'm really grateful, Jack. Thank you so much. For believing in me and helping me".

"It's my pleasure," says Jack. "It's been fun. And I hope that we have many more runs together. Now, let's go get ourselves scanned before we forget and they think we've run off home with the finish tokens.

We headed back to the crowds at the finish area and handed over our personal barcode and then our finish tokens to get scanned. I finished in 65th place which was the highest placing I had ever finished by a long way.

There was no way I was running home though. I was absolutely beaten.

Jack headed off to find his bike which he had ridden from home as he'd been running a bit late. We bid farewell and had already arranged to meet up tonight, just the two of us for dinner. We had said that we might meet up with Molly & Harry after that, but we wanted to spend a little time on our own initially.

As I started walking out of the park, James sauntered up to me. I hadn't seen him for the whole of parkrun, and he told me that he had run a quick one in around 21 minutes. That would explain why I didn't see him. He asked how I got on and I proudly told him that I had achieved a new PB in around 26:10 and that I was excited for the results to come out a little later on. He seemed to be truly happy for me.

James then asked what I was up to this evening. I explained that I was going for dinner with Jack, and that we might catch up with Molly and Harry later on. I asked what he was doing. He said that he was spending the afternoon with Jasmine and that they would go from there. He has no specific plans for this evening at the moment, but assumed he would still be with Jazz.

We bid farewell and I headed home for a shower and a much needed chill out day.

Chapter 24

Although it wasn't a special occasion, the fact that Jack & I were off out to dinner alone made me want to make a bit of an effort. It wasn't a regular occurrence for me to wear a dress, but I decided that I wanted to today.

My favourite dress was a black dress with flowers on it. It was a nice, light material, and clung to my curves in the right places. It was sexy but sophisticated. I had some silver sandals to wear with it, and I arranged to borrow a silver clutch off Mum. I didn't usually carry a handbag of any type, but it would be convenient to have somewhere to put some cash, a card and a couple of other bits and pieces. Normally I'd wear jeans or cargo pants which have pockets of course.

Once I'd showered and dressed, I put on minimal makeup. I didn't usually wear makeup, but just used a little today to accentuate my features. Mum kindly offered to straighten my hair, so I did actually feel pretty fabulous. This wasn't a feeling that I was particularly used to.

At seven on the dot Jack arrived. Mum invited him in and offered to open a bottle of Sauvignon Blanc. The three of us then picked up the wine glasses that she poured and we went into the lounge. We had a nice, easy chat between the three of us, talking about swimming in the river and the nice weather that we were enjoying. Mum used to swim in the river all year round, and was telling us about the physical and mental benefits of open water swimming. I'm not sure that I fancy it in the winter time although it's great fun in the summer. Soon enough, we had polished off the wine and it was time for Jack and I to leave.

Jack had booked us a table at an Italian Restaurant about ten minutes' drive away. He'd decided he'd drive us there and then we could get a taxi back at the end of the evening. His car would be quite safe until the morning when he'd pop back to fetch it. As we arrived, the waiter showed us to a table in the corner of a really beautiful, authentically decorated Italian restaurant. It was a family owned establishment, so the waiters, waitress, chefs and barman were all from the same Italian family. They'd been in the UK for two generations and the restaurant has an amazing reputation.

Jack ordered us another bottle of Sauvignon Blanc and we began to peruse the menu. Oh my, it looked amazing. My mouth was watering just reading about the dishes and looking at some of the pictures. However, as a creature of habit, I decided to order a salad dish to start which was avocado, mozzarella and tomatoes with olive oil, vinaigrette and sea salt. For mains I was going to have a grilled steak, with thinly shaved Parmigiano Reggiano and a drizzle of extra virgin olive oil and balsamic vinegar. This was served with dauphinois potatoes, tomato and some vegetables. It sounded absolutely divine.

Jack ordered some kind of sausage starter, and then a chicken risotto dish. The lovely waitress turned up with our wine, poured us a glass each and then provided us with an ice bucket for the rest of the bottle. I was absolutely starving, and couldn't wait for the first course to arrive.

Jack and I had some general chit chat talking about our day. I didn't mention the conversation that I had with James. Not because it was a secret or anything like that, but just that I was truly enjoying the lovely, relaxed atmosphere between us and I didn't want to change that. We laughed, we talked, we held hands. I felt really close to Jack and enjoyed his company very much. Whilst we hadn't known each other very long, it had been quite action packed, and we'd had a lot of fun. I felt like the relationship was a little on fast forward. Even though we had only spent a few weeks together, I felt like I had known Jack for much longer than that. I felt a really strong pull towards him – I felt comfortable with him but there was also an exciting spark between us.

Our starters arrived, and we both enjoyed them whilst sipping at our wine. It was nice that Jack enjoyed alcohol, but didn't seem to drink it too quickly or let it go to his head. He also kept our water glasses topped up, and just seemed to get mellow rather than affected by the alcohol. It was a big difference from Rob, who didn't seem to have a stop button when it came to alcohol. Once he started drinking you could pretty much guarantee he'd only stop when he fell into bed. And he often became obnoxious after a few drinks. I'd seen no evidence of that with Jack – he really did seem to keep that lovely character the whole time.

I'd been trying not to get too excited about Jack. But he really did seem to tick every box for 'life partner' that I had in my head. The more that I got to know him, the more I liked him. I truly felt like I was falling for him. When I wasn't with him, I was thinking about him. I just hoped that he felt the same about me.

Our main courses soon arrived. They looked amazing. Soon, there was just a comfortable silence between us as we both started eating. It was nice that

132

neither of us felt the need to fill in the conversation gap. We were quite happy just enjoying each other's company and concentrated on the food that had arrived.

The steak was absolutely amazing. It was like an explosion of flavours in my mouth. There is nothing special about the way that Italians prepare their food, but if you try and recreate it at home it just never tastes the same. I guess that's where skill comes into it. My culinary skills are pretty limited, so nothing ever tastes as good as it should when I've cooked it. It does also seem that if someone else cooks food it tastes better than if you've done it yourself. Couple the amazing food with a beautiful tasting wine and great company, and I felt truly happy.

As we were eating our mains, we discussed where we would go next. I knew that Molly & Harry were in a bar at the other end of town, and I was quite liking the idea of going to join them. Jack seemed open to the idea, so I sent a text to Molly to check that they were still there. She replied that they would be there for at least the next hour, so I said we'd go and join them soon.

When we had finished our food (not a crumb was left) and drained the wine, Jack paid the bill. I offered to pay half but he wouldn't entertain the idea. I agreed on condition that I got the first round at the bar. And I also left a £10 cash tip which would later be divided amongst all the staff on duty that evening. The waiter was extremely grateful for the tip. It seems since most people pay by card nowadays the tip often gets overlooked.

As we left the restaurant, with promises to go back again soon, Jack took hold of my arm, and we started walking across town. It was a nice, warm evening and I felt happy and relaxed, enjoying Jack's company and looking forward to seeing Molly.

As we stepped off a kerb to cross the road, I felt this sharp pain behind my knee. My legs went from underneath me, somebody barged into the side of me, and I felt the clutch bag being ripped from my shoulder. I grabbed at the bag with my hand and felt myself being pulled along. I looked up to see a man in a black hoodie pulling hard at my bag strap. I was still holding onto Jack as he clocked what was happening. He let go of me to run at the man attempting to steal my bag. The man in the hoodie immediately let going of my bag, resulting in me ending up falling into the gutter on the side of the road. The man ran incredibly fast away from us, with Jack sprinting after him for a few paces. Jack then span around and ran back to me, helping me up from the gutter in the road. A passing car had also stopped to make sure that I was alright and they left their details with us as a potential witness.

The would-be thief was long gone by this time. There were a few people milling about but aside from the car witness and a lady behind us, no-one else had seen anything. Unfortunately, I didn't really see much aside from black jeans, black trainers and a black hoodie, and Jack and the other witnesses couldn't really add much either. We had all really only seen the back or side of him. The car driver had seen the front of him, but said because his hood was up he couldn't actually see any of his features, and could only add that he had dark hair and wasn't wearing glasses. We all thought he was about 6 foot tall.

We took the lady witness details as well, and informed her and the car driver that we would hand their details to the police. To be honest, I doubt they would do anything as it was only attempted theft. The man with the hoodie didn't actually get away with anything, as James had been so quick to react, and I had refused to immediately let go of the bag. As we were only a couple of streets from the police station, we walked there and reported the details to the police. They did give us an incident number, but it was clear that no further action would be taken. The policeman did explain that with such a limited description of the would-be thief, and the fact that nothing was taken, it wasn't a high priority enough to investigate. The limited resources would be better used elsewhere so it seems.

By now, another hour had passed, and I really didn't feel up to staying out. So Jack walked me home quietly. I had texted Molly to let her know what had happened and why we hadn't turned up. She was disappointed that we wouldn't get to catch up, but understood that I was a little shaken up and just wanted to go home.

When we got home, Mum was already in bed, so I asked Jack if he wanted to stay the night. He worried about Mum, but I assured him that she wouldn't mind, especially in view of what had happened and that I was quite scared. It reassured me to know that Jack would be by my side throughout the night. Plus, we hadn't yet had sex, and I was pretty damn keen to do so. Hopefully this would be my opportunity.

I opened the fridge, and as luck would have it there was an opened bottle of wine. I grabbed two glasses from the cupboard and poured us both a generous amount of wine, way beyond the amount that you get served in a pub. It was either that or leave a pathetically poor amount left in the bottle which seemed ridiculous.

We headed upstairs. Luckily my bedroom is the other side of the house to Mums, so I wasn't too worried about waking her. We entered my room and put our glasses down by the side of the bed. Jack then put his hands on my shoulders and turned me to face him before kissing me deeply. He cupped his hand behind my head and stroked down my neck whilst kissing me. He then ran his hand down my front, lightly cupping my breast as he went. He continued to run his hand down to my waist and then snaking behind to stroke my ass. He pulled me towards him until I was pressed up against him such that I could feel his hard on through his trousers.

I put my arm around his back and ran my hand down his strong, broad back. I then felt the shape of his ass and pulled him hard onto me. He gently walked forwards, pushing me backwards until I sat on the edge of the bed. He continue to push on my shoulders until I was lying down on the bed, and then we both swivelled around until we were lying down the bed, rather than across it.

"I can't believe it's taken us this long to get into bed," I whispered. "I've been dying to get to know you further, and haven't really had the chance – other than in a tent when it was way too cold to consider leaving my sleeping bag."

"Well, hopefully it will have been worth the wait," replied Jack. "You have no idea how much I want you right now. However, this damn dress is doing my head in."

Jack had been fumbling about with my dress, not sure how to take it off. I laughed, and sat up lifting my hips so that Jack could slide the dress up around my waist. I

136

then lifted my arms so that he could continue to take the dress off over my head.

"That's better," he sighed. "Wow. You are just beautiful. I love the lingerie."

I wasn't usually a lingerie kind of girl, but I had recently bought a rather nice red bra & thong set which I had worn under my dress. It did actually make me feel really sexy and I felt glad that I'd made the effort with my outfit tonight. Lying in my bra & thong, I felt amazing. It was so good knowing that Jack was really attracted to me. It gave me a real warm buzz. It also made me feel super horny. And the bonus of lying down meant that I looked slim. You could even see some definition in my abs, courtesy of my recent running routine.

Now however, I wanted to check Jack out properly. I started unbuttoning his shirt and then his jeans. He shrugged himself out of his shirt, and then lifted his hips so that I could slide off his trousers. Jack was slim, broad, quite muscley and a great set of abs. I wanted to slide my tongue over his stomach so much.

"Don't forget the socks," Jack smirked.

He was right. There is nothing worse than a fit man, down to his boxers in bed, still wearing his socks. Off came the socks, and for good measure, I threw them across the room.

We'd broken the tension slightly so I reached up and took hold of the wine glasses.

"I want to savour this time with you," I rather huskily whispered to Jack. "There is no hurry. Let's take our time and really enjoy the moment."

"Trust me," replied Jack. "I fully intend to savour every second."

He had a bit of a wicked glint in his eye. We both sipped at our wine whilst looking into each other's eyes. I felt that butterfly feeling in my stomach. I felt truly comfortable, happy and excited to spend the night with Jack.

Wine glasses down, Jack reached for me again. He pulled me down until I was straddled over him. I could feel his hard on through my knickers. I knew how horny I was feeling and knew that I would already be incredibly moist for him.

I leant forward and we kissed. He cupped my breast and rolled me over until he was straddling me, and I was lying on my back. He started to kiss by my ear, and I could feel his warm breath which made the butterflies return with a vengeance. He laid a trail of kisses down my neck, over my collar bone, down to my breast. He sucked gently on my nipple and circled it with his tongue. He continued down and I could feel him kissing my stomach, past my belly button and continuing down to my core.

He gently pushed my legs apart, and started to tease me with his tongue. Thank god I had shaved so there was no hair. The warmth of his breath and the softness of his tongue literally took my breath away. He was so gentle and it felt so sensuous. All I could feel was my inner voice saying 'please put your finger inside me. Please put your finger inside me'. I was so horny, there would certainly be no need for any lubricant. I wasn't moist, I was positively wet, and he hadn't even entered a finger into me yet.

Jack continued to lick around my clitoris, and his finger teased my vaginal opening. My inner voice was begging him to slide a finger inside me. He lapped gently at

138

me with his tongue, and gradually, slowly, oh so slowly, started to push a finger into my warmth. I lifted my hips, almost sliding onto his finger myself. I was that desperate to feel him inside me. Finally, he allowed his finger to enter me fully. I was so wet it was almost embarrassing. But I could tell that he was enjoying himself too.

I squeezed my inner muscles, tightening around his finger.

"You feel amazing," whispered Jack. "You are so warm & wet. I love it."

By now Jack was gently but deeply moving two fingers inside of me whilst still licking my clitoris.

"I will not last more than seconds like this Jack. It's pure ecstasy," I responded.

I had slept with a handful of men over the years, but not many compared to some. But nothing had ever felt like this. Previously, especially on the first time with a new partner, it all seemed a bit hurried and practical. This was totally different. It was like we were just in tune. Jack seemed to know to be gentle but probing with his tongue and his fingers.

By now my inner voice was clamouring at me again. 'You need him inside you. You want him inside you. Please, I want to climb on top of you.'

Suddenly, I realised that my inner voice had failed me. I had actually just whispered to Jack

"Please, I want to climb on top of you".

"Don't let me stop you," replied Jack. "I can't wait to be inside you. Wait though, I just need to grab a condom".

With that Jack leant over to his jeans and slid a condom out of the back pocket. I was very glad that he was prepared. Jack used his teeth to open the wrapper, while still caressing me. And he then slid the condom onto his hard cock.

I climbed over him until I straddled him, and I bent down to kiss him some more. I moved my hand down and for the first time felt how large Jack's cock was. There was certainly no danger of him not being hard enough. He felt solid as a rock.

I guided the end of his cock over my opening and I scooched my knees apart a little more until his tip entered me. And then I stopped. I could see the desire making Jack's eyes sparkle even more than normal. He lifted his hips up to enter me a little more, but I made sure to match his movement so that he just stayed at the tip depth. I continued to kiss him while staring into his eyes. There was so much emotion and feeling in that look.

Millimetre by millimetre I lowered myself down a little. I could feel my opening stretch to accommodate his rock hard cock. I felt an amazing feeling spread throughout my body. It was like a tingling or buzzing sensation that started from my core and spread outwards. Finally, I was fully lowered and his cock was buried deep inside me. I stayed still just enjoying the moment.

I started to move, just a few millimetres and squeezing my inner muscles against him. I could feel the effect that it had on him.

"Oh my god, how do you even do that?" Jack asked.

"Sssshhhhh," I said. "Just enjoy."

I felt pure happiness, total emotion and also an element of power. I felt that Jack was totally at my mercy. Whilst in no way was I dominating him, I was certainly in control of things and making him dance to my beat. Which currently was very, very slow and sensual. This wasn't sex. It was lovemaking. It felt like there was an amazing connection between the two of us.

I took hold of his wrists, and I pushed them down against the pillow. Another day, I fully had plans to tie him up with some silk scarves, and take great pleasure in playing with him until he begged me to take him inside of me. Today though, I had a little more urgency, although I was trying hard to take it slowly. I wanted tonight to be memorable for the right reasons.

"Please," begged Jack. "I need you now. I can't wait anymore."

"Me too," I replied. "Me too."

And with that I began to grind down on him. Still slowly, but so very, very deeply. It became a little more rhythmic and we moved together as if we had been having sex for years. There was no awkwardness, nothing except passion.

I could feel Jack lifting his hips so that I could take him even deeper, if that were even possible. I could feel the orgasm begin to rise, and take over, so that I started to lose control. The rhythm quickened and the beautiful sensation flooded through me. I heard Jack gasp, and then he gave a moan.

I could feel the climax was coming and it seemed that Jack was going to orgasm at the same time. We did indeed both cum together and as the shuddering from us both died down, I suddenly felt absolutely exhausted. I collapsed onto Jack's chest and he wrapped his arms around me. We just laid together, totally spent, in each other's arms.

Jack reached down and held the condom whilst I inched off of him. I rolled over to his side and he sat up slightly to tie the top of the condom and place it on the floor beside the bed. He then lay back down and I snuggled up against him, one leg over his. Our breathing shallowed and my racing heart returned back to normal. I felt this feeling of total contentment wash over me. I felt so happy and so connected with Jack. It really had been amazing.

But now, I needed to sleep. With the busy week, the events of the night and then having sex with Jack for the first time, I was absolutely done. I could feel my eyes were already closing and Jack hugged me to him while the two of us drifted off to sleep.

Chapter 25

Surprisingly, we woke up before 7am the next morning. As I couldn't hear Mum stirring yet, Jack decided to leave to avoid the inevitable questions. I went downstairs in my dressing gown, and Jack slipped quietly out of the door and headed home. I relocked the door, then went back to bed and managed to sleep for a couple more hours.

The next time I woke, the house was full of the beautiful smells of breakfast. Namely, bacon and eggs. What a star my Mum is. One of the perks of living back at home for a little while. I jumped quickly in the shower and then headed downstairs where Mum had eggs, bacon, tomatoes and hash browns waiting for me. I made us some toast to go with it, and we sat down companionably to eat.

"So how was your evening?" Mum asked.

"Eventful." I replied.

I then filled Mum in starting with the details of our romantic dinner, the attempted mugging and the following trip to the police station.

"I know that Jack came back and stayed with you last night," said Mum. "It's not an issue. You are a perfectly grown woman. You didn't have to sneak him out this morning."

"I know," I laughed. "But staying here somehow makes me feel guilty. It's because I haven't lived at home since I was 17 I think. I wasn't really sneaking him out, but it just seemed like it would avoid too many questions".

"Well, next time get him to stay for breakfast. There is no need for him to rush off," replied Mum.

"Thank you," I replied. "I'm really grateful. I won't rush him off next time."

We continued eating and chatting about the day ahead. I was planning on having a bit of a chill day. The weather today was a bit poor, so I had a couple of things that I wanted to watch on Netflix. I planned to snuggle up on the sofa with some biscuits and just relax.

"What are you planning for your birthday?" asked Mum.

"I have no idea," I replied. "I've not really thought about it. I suppose I should do something really seeing as it's my 30th."

My birthday is the weekend after next. I'd have to catch up with Molly and see what she wanted to do.

Chapter 26

The weekend before my birthday ended up being a quiet one as Jack was away on a stag do. This was the first of four stag do's that he is committed to this year. I guess that at our age a lot of people are getting married. It does occasionally make me think that I need to get a move on. No pressure then. Jack's only complaint is that whilst they are good fun, they are not cheap, and he's trying to save some money too.

Saturday night I went over for a girlie night in with Molly. We were planning on drinking wine, watching a movie and having a good catch up. We also were going to finalise what we were going to do for my birthday.

It is of a bit of a milestone turning 30. However, as I don't want to be spending too much money, many of my initial ideas are deemed too expensive.

I really fancy wing walking. This is where you get strapped onto the wing of a light aircraft while it flies. It would be amazingly scary and exhilarating. Molly said that she would cheer me on but that there was absolutely no chance of her doing it with me. She is scared of heights and is not big on adventure. However, after a bit of research I discarded the idea for the moment. There are very limited organisations that offer this activity in the UK and it's incredibly expensive. Certainly not something to be done at this point in my life.

As I'm getting a little older now, I did contemplate holding a dinner party. But the drawbacks of that are the fact that I don't like cooking, and that the only place big enough to hold a decent number of people would be Mum's house, and I didn't really feel comfortable with that. It wasn't really fair on Mum.

Molly suggested having a party in one of the pubs or bars. I like that idea but have a concern that if I pay to secure a private room, only a few people might turn up and I end up looking like Billy No Mates. If I don't have a private area then the pub might be super busy with people that I don't know. Either way it could either cost me too much money or there be too many/too few people.

Agh! It's so difficult to decide what to do.

After debating the pro's and con's and going around in a number of circles, I finally make a decision. I decide that I would like to do a fun activity in the daytime with just the four of us. I'd then like to go for a nice meal with just the four of us, and then head to the cocktail bar and see if my closest friends want to join us there. To be honest, the only people I'm really concerned about sharing the day or evening with are Jack, Molly, Harry, Georgia and Evie. I think as you get older you realise that what is important is the quality of friendships that you have, rather than the quantity of friends.

Molly agreed that was a good plan of action, so that is what we settled on. Molly said that she would sort out the day's activities, she would get the guys to sort the meal out and I would contact Georgia and Evie to see if they'd join us in the cocktail bar afterwards. This seemed a great solution, and wouldn't cost me too much money.

We started debating what movie to watch and whether to open another bottle of wine. We had already finished a bottle of sauvignon blanc that Molly already had. The next bottle I had picked up from the off licence on the way over. Molly started opening the bottle as the doorbell rang, so she handed it to me to finish while she went to the door.

"Are you expecting anyone else Molly?" I asked.

"No," she replied. "I have no idea who it could be. Maybe it's just a delivery."

Molly opened the door and I could hear another female voice, but I didn't recognise who it was. Molly came back into the lounge and I was surprised to see Jasmine following her.

"Oh hello Lily," said Jasmine. "I didn't realise you were here. I didn't mean to interrupt anything."

"No problem," I replied rather awkwardly.

"Sit down," said Molly. "Can I get you a glass of wine Jasmine?"

"No thank you," replied Jasmine. "I'm not stopping and I'm driving anyway. I just wanted to ask your advice about something but I didn't realise that you had company and I don't want to intrude."

"What can I help you with?" asked Molly politely.

"Well, it's a bit awkward now," said Jasmine. "I wanted to ask you something about James."

"Don't mind me," I said. "I was actually going to pop out to the shop on the corner and get some ice-cream. You ladies chat, and I'll let myself out and be back in about ten minutes."

"Are you sure?" asked Jasmine. "I feel really awkward now."

"Please don't," I reassured her. "I'll be back shortly."

With that I jumped up, popped on my shoes and headed out of the flat. I wandered down to the corner shop, bought some mint choc chip ice-cream and then headed back. I perched outside on the wall for a few minutes to give them enough time to finish their chat.

As I headed up the stairs to the flat, I heard Molly's door open, and Jasmine saying goodbye and thank you to Molly. We passed each other on the stairs and said goodbye.

I headed back into the flat, popped the ice-cream into the freezer and took a big slug from my glass of wine.

"What was that all about?" I asked Molly.

"Well, probably not surprising that she wanted to talk about James. And of course your name came up too."

"In what context?" I asked.

"Apparently, things aren't too good between her and James. She says that he is distant and she doesn't feel like he is that interested in her anymore. She says it's really different to how they were before she went to the States."

"But that's to be expected, surely," I remark. "She was gone for two years. A lot changes in two years. People change."

"I think she worries about you. He's told her that he was really enjoying getting to know you and that it took him a long time to move on when she left, but that he had moved on. And now he feels like he's taking a step back in time. And doesn't feel that that's necessarily the right thing to do."

"I do feel for both of them," I said. "It is a difficult situation. I really liked James, but I've moved on now. We weren't together long enough for too many feelings to develop. And as Jack turned up straight afterwards it wasn't too difficult to accept that our relationship was over.

148

"I think Jasmine was worried that maybe Jack was seeing you behind her back," replied Molly. "And that was why he wasn't committed to their relationship. I was at least able to reassure her that that isn't the case, and that you had moved on. Of course, James might still have feelings for you as you can't necessarily just switch them off, but you certainly aren't doing anything to undermine their relationship. I think she left feeling a bit better about things. If things don't work out between her and James, it's not because of anything that you are actively doing."

"Well, I like to think that I'm not that sort of girl anyway. Even if I was single, I would have taken a step back and given them the space to figure things out either way. It just gets messy otherwise and that's not something that I'm interested in doing. I wouldn't want it done to me, and I like to treat others as I like to be treated."

"I agree," said Molly. "But we are probably in the minority. Most girls wouldn't think twice about treading on someone else's toes. But at the end of the day, it will either work out for them or it won't. I always think you are better off knowing the truth rather than trying to drag out something that clearly isn't working."

"Indeed," I agreed. "Anyway, I suggest we get on with drinking the wine, have a bowl of ice-cream each, and watch a movie."

"Deal," said Molly.

The conversation continued with what movie to choose. In the end we went with Bad Moms which we both wanted to watch. It's a comedy with Mila Kunis and even though we don't yet have kids, we still thought it was a great movie and enjoyed the rest of a very pleasant evening.

Chapter 27

The dawn of my 30th birthday heralded a beautiful day of sunshine and little, fluffy clouds. I woke up, pulled back my curtains and lay in bed thinking of the song by The Orb 'Little Fluffy Clouds'. It reminded me of my late teens when I was at University.

I felt really happy. Things had been going well with Jack. He's stayed over with me a few nights now – and even stayed for breakfast with Mum. I was starting to feel settled and happy.

Molly and I had been chatting about my birthday plans some more over the last week. Some of our other friends were going to join us after dinner to celebrate my birthday too. Hopefully Evie & Georgia would make it out, as they hadn't yet met Jack. Now that it seemed that Jack was going to be a long-term (possibly permanent) fixture in my life, I wanted him to meet everyone that was important to me.

I hadn't yet met Jack's family, but we were planning to go and visit them in a couple of weeks' time. We'd even loosely talked about moving in together in the not so distant future. Exciting times. Anyway, time to get out of bed and start enjoying my birthday.

I headed downstairs and shared breakfast with Mum. As we were finishing Molly turned up. We'd decided that we were going to make the most of the glorious sunshine and go to the river. Jack had a small dinghy and Harry had an inflatable. And us girls were making a picnic. Molly and I made some sandwiches and packed up some sausage rolls, pork pies, some dips and crisps. We also had some fruit, carrot, cucumber sticks and even managed to find some strawberries so we could at least pretend to be a little bit healthy.

Jack and Harry were bringing some drinks and we were going to a picnic area at the river just a few miles away. Mum kindly did the rounds to pick everyone up and then dropped us off so that we could have a few alcoholic drinks. We also had the picnic basket, a couple of blankets, some paper plates and plastic glasses. We were planning to be at least semi-civilised.

The boys had become firm friends over the handful of times that they had met. It was really nice spending time as a group rather than just a couple. It was so different to Rob, who only ever wanted to spend time by ourselves. The boys had a cool box which held a couple of bottles of bubbles (admittedly cava rather than champagne, not that many can tell the difference), some cider (they had my name on), some lager, some orange juice and diet coke.

The river was a popular area and today there were a dozen or so kids already present. A couple of them I knew by sight, so they popped over to say hi and happy birthday.

We laid out the picnic blanket, the basket of food, and the boys opened up the first bottle of cava. I pulled out some plastic champagne flutes, and we all relaxed once they had been filled. We had a laugh and a giggle while enjoying the sunshine and watched the kids splash about in the water. The boys then inflated the dingy and the inflatable dinosaur (you couldn't make it up) and we decided to brave the water.

"My god it's FREEZING" shouted Molly. "How on earth do some people do this all year round?"

She'd only got in as far as her waist. I waded in to catch her up. I always enjoyed swimming in the river, and to me it didn't feel too bad – once you'd got over the initial shock of course. Within a minute or so of entering the water I was happily swimming across to the other bank.

The boys had launched the dingy off the side, and Molly decided that was a better option than having a swim. She scurried back out of the water and flopped herself into the dingy. Harry was already in the dingy and rowing it out into the river. The river at this point was a good 150 feet wide, so there was plenty of room for us, the dingy and all the other kids.

At that point Jack came over to me in the water, half atop the dinosaur. I burst out laughing because he looked so comical particularly as he couldn't really balance on the dinosaur properly and kept sliding off.

"Ever snogged a dinosaur?" Jack questioned whilst laughing.

"No," I responded. "But I'd like to give it a go."

Instead, I reached over, pulled the dinosaur towards me and gave Jack a lingering kiss on the lips. He promptly slithered off the dinosaur into the water, and handed the inflatable to me.

I tried to climb onto the dinosaur, but it was too wet and slippy to get on, so Jack helped me with a boost at the ankle enabling me to scramble on in a very unladylike fashion. Once aboard, I seemed to have a little more balance than Jack and stayed more or less on top of the dinosaur. That is until Jack grabbed my leg and pulled me off straight under the water. Caught unawares, I came up spluttering and coughing.

152

"Do you want to join me in the dingy?" asked Molly.

"I will a bit later," I replied. "I'm quite enjoying my dinosaur right now thank you".

Actually, I was starting to feel a little cold. Whilst it was fun, I needed to get out before I got too cold and stopped enjoying myself. I headed for the bank and scrambled up and walked over to the picnic blanket. I carefully retrieved my glass of cava, of which I'd only drunk half, and started sipping again. I was already drying off and warming up in the beautiful sunshine.

Molly came to join me carrying the dinosaur, leaving the boys with the dingy. They informed us that they were going to have a little row upstream, so they set off leaving Molly and I with a bit of peace and quiet for a chat.

"So how's things going?" Molly asked.

"Good," I replied. "Really good. We seem to have settled into a really nice relationship. Jack has spent a few nights at Mum's house with me now, and we've loosely talked about moving in together in the not too distant future."

"Wow," replied Molly. "That's a bit full on. You've only been together a few weeks."

"I know, but it just seems to work and I really do need to move out from Mum's and Jack's flat is not in a great location for him, so he's quite keen to move too. Jack lived with a mate previously which worked well for him, but he moved out and was replaced by a guy that Jack doesn't really gel with, so he's not really got anything keeping him where he is," I replied. "How about you and Harry? Have you talked about living together?"

"Well, we have rather loosely," said Molly. "But Harry loves living with James, and he doesn't really know what's going on with him at the moment, so he doesn't want to make any big changes right now".

"What do you mean? What's wrong with James" I asked.

"He's not in a good place at the moment. I didn't tell you this, but I think he's regretting getting back with Jasmine and losing you. He's definitely not happy," replied Molly.

I hadn't heard anything about James for a couple of weeks, and to be honest, I hadn't really thought about him. The last time I saw him was in the park where he told me that things weren't going great, but I hadn't heard from him since so had more or less forgotten about him. Of course, as things were going so well with Jack, it was natural that I hadn't thought about him much.

At that point the boys returned, and they dragged the dinghy out of the water after confirming that Molly & I didn't want to use it at the moment. Harry then asked Molly to go for a little stroll with him as he wanted to show her something a little further upstream. So Molly scrambled up and Jack dropped down beside me.

He lay down next to me and took hold of my hand.

"Lily sweetheart. I'm so enjoying spending time with you and getting to know you. I really miss you when I'm not with you now," Jack stated.

"I know exactly how you feel," I responded. "I'm so falling for you Jack. I love the time that we spend together. I enjoy chilling with you, I enjoy going out with you, I enjoy running with you. I just enjoy being with you, regardless of what we do".

"I'm the same Lily," confirmed Jack. "I'm totally falling in love with you."

I rolled over onto my side, propped myself up on my elbow, and gazed deep into Jack's eyes. They were mesmerising and I could lose myself in his eyes forever.

"Me too Jack," I murmured. "Me too."

Jack reached for me and pulled me down onto his chest. I rested my head on him and relaxed, enjoying the warmth, the closeness and the feeling of the sun beating down on us. I felt truly happy. We lay for a few minutes without talking. I was enjoying just listening to his heartbeat and feeling his chest expand and contract as he breathed. It was so nice to just be in the moment. To just be.

I was just starting to drift off when I heard Molly and Harry return. They were laughing and holding hands.

"For goodness sake you two," Harry laughed. "Haven't you opened the other bottle of cava yet?"

"We were just chilling," replied Jack. "I'll open it now though.

Jack reached over and opened the other bottle of cava. He gathered up the four flutes and poured the cava into them. Molly & Harry joined us on the blanket and Jack made a toast.

"To friendship and to love," he said with a wink at me.

"To friendship and love" we all chanted back.

The four of us continued to enjoy the sunshine and chat together, and time passed by. After the cava the boys had a couple of beers each, I had a cider and Molly drank some Bucks Fizz. Soon, it was time to leave if we wanted to get dressed up and out for dinner tonight.

Chapter 28

The boys had booked a surprise meal out for my birthday dinner. All that we had been told was that we were to dress up. Mum had kindly offered to pick us all up from the river and drop us home to enable us to all get ready to go out, saving us from having to leave cars anywhere.

A couple of hours later, Molly and I were showered and dressed up ready to leave.

"Come on then Lily, give us a twirl," requested Molly.

I had borrowed a really beautiful red, light summer dress from Molly. She has a much better selection of clothes to choose from than I do. The dress was stunning and I felt pretty awesome when it was on. I did a full 360 degree twirl for Molly and the dress flared up nicely. It was a nice mix of sexy, summery yet sophisticated. It was also comfortable which was an added bonus. I had a pair of silver sandals to wear with it that I had borrowed from Mum. Luckily, we had a similar size foot so I was able to borrow shoes from her on occasion.

Mum had once again offered to drive us to the venue, so she had been kept in the loop as to our destination even though I hadn't. The three of us jumped into the car and off we went.

Mum pulled up at a very reputable steakhouse about 15 minutes' drive away. I'd only eaten here once before, a few years back, and it was wonderful. My mouth started to water at the thought of it. I love steak, even though I didn't get to eat the good stuff very often.

We said goodbye to Mum and she wished us a happy evening. Molly & I then entered the steakhouse and found the boys sitting at the bar area near the entrance. There was a nice buzzing atmosphere inside and nearly all of the tables were already full.

"What would you like to drink ladies?" Harry asked. Both him and Jack stood up to give us both a kiss.

"Well, seeing as it's Lily's birthday today, I think we had better order some bubbles," said Molly.

"Don't order champagne though," I requested. "Let's stick to cava or prosecco. It's just as nice and only a third of the price, so we can enjoy more of it without feeling guilty."

"Good plan," replied Jack. "I'll happily drink cava with you. It makes a nice change from lager."

Harry agreed, so the barman opened up a bottle of cava and poured out four glasses for us. We'd been told that our table would be about 15 minutes yet and as such the first bottle of cava was on the house. That was a result.

A short time later we were shown to our table, and menus were handed to us. Despite eating some of the picnic this afternoon I felt absolutely starving. We decided to have some sharing starters and then we could all try a few different dishes.

As we were enjoying the various starters that we had received, a rose seller came around touting for business.

"I'll definitely have one of those please," said Jack. "It's my girlfriends birthday today. A rose would be lovely to give her".

I felt really spoilt and really happy. Jack handed me the most beautiful red rose.

"Red for love," whispered Jack to me as he kissed me on the lips. "Happy Birthday sweetheart. I look forward to spending many more birthdays with you."

It felt really romantic, even having Molly and Harry with us. Molly has been beside me for so many years, she is such a big part of my life. It felt great to share the happy moments with her. And I really liked Harry too. He is a lovely man, clearly devoted to Molly, and I was truly happy that we had both met great men at a similar time and could share the good times with each other.

Jack then turned away from me slightly and started fiddling in his jacket pocket. He turned back to me with a beautifully wrapped box, about the size of a jewellery box. My heart started to race a little, even though I knew it was far too early in our relationship to be thinking about diamonds. But, I did have a habit occasionally of rushing a little bit too quick into relationships, and I couldn't help the thoughts that popped into my head.

"Happy Birthday Lily. I hope you like it" said Jack.

I took the box from him, said thank you, and started to unwrap the paper. It was indeed a jewellery box, although a little larger than a ring box. I gently opened the box and saw two beautiful silver earrings with what looked like diamonds in them. The label on the box said 'Argentium' so I asked Jack what that meant.

"Argentium is a new type of metal. It's a silver alloy. Normal silver tarnishes over time, but Argentium does not so it will stay its current sparkling silver colour over time. And, I hate to disappoint but the diamonds are not diamonds," explained Jack. "They are cubic zirconia. But I loved the earrings and thought that you would like

158

them too. I'd like to have bought you diamonds, but I thought it was more important to save up for a house deposit with you than spend money on jewellery at this stage in our relationship."

I did love the earrings. They were elegant, classy, small and beautiful. I am really not a fan of large earrings, and Jack had chosen perfectly. I leant over and gave him a big kiss on the lips while thanking him at the same time.

"They are gorgeous," cooed Molly. "You are lucky."

"Indeed I am," I replied. "Thank you so much Jack. I'm so grateful. They are a lovely gift, and I feel totally spoilt."

The starters were cleared away and the main course arrived. It was absolutely divine. I had chosen a steak dish again. The steak literally melted in my mouth and was so beautifully flavoursome. The grilled tomato tasted amazing, there were chips done just how I liked them and some salad with the most gorgeous vinaigrette dressing. There was even some garlic mushrooms included which added a nice additional flavour and some creamed spinach. It was all truly fantastic.

We laughed and chatted, and steadily worked our way through a second bottle of cava. We were all feeling merry, but nobody was out of control or seeming drunk (at this stage anyway.). It was a thoroughly enjoyable evening.

I couldn't really fit in a full dessert, but Jack had apparently provided some small chocolate cupcakes which each had a candle stuck in them. As the waiter brought them over to us, he lit a couple of sparklers and the whole restaurant sang happy birthday to me. Despite being a little embarrassed, it was a really nice touch. I don't really like most cakes, and it was so thoughtful that Jack had remembered what I do like and brought them for me. I was really touched at the gesture. It's the little things that matter, rather than big extravagant presents.

By the time we had finished our cupcakes, finished the bubbles and paid up (the boys kindly split the bill between the pair of them) it was past ten o'clock. We were heading into the cocktail bar that we liked to go to sometimes. Hopefully Georgia & Evie were going to meet us.

Chapter 29

Ten minutes later we walked into the bar, and I was happy to see that Georgia & Evie were already there. The bar was busy, so as Georgia was near the front of the crowd at the bar, I shouted across asking her to add our drinks to her order. I tried to hand her enough money to cover our drinks, but she brushed it away.

There wasn't anywhere to sit, so we perched against a ledge running along the wall which enabled us to at least put our drinks down. Georgia & Evie gave me a massive hug and wished me a happy birthday. Molly and I had a cocktail made of prosecco and a blackcurrant liqueur. It looked and tasted spectacular.

I introduced Jack to Georgia and Evie, and I could see that they immediately warmed to him. As well as being very handsome, Jack is of course very charming and friendly. And the girls were enjoying having a chat with him. Typically, they were soon asking him if he had any nice single friends.

A few minutes later, I headed off to the ladies, with Molly in tow. Just as I was about to head into the toilets, I felt a tug on my arm. I turned around and standing there was Rob. Now that was a surprise. And he had a smile on his face. It had been a couple of months since I last saw Rob, and he hadn't even entered my thoughts for many weeks.

"Happy Birthday Lily," Rob slurred. "I thought you might be in here tonight. Is it just you and Molly tonight?"

I saw Molly give me the 'are you alright' look, and I nodded back to reassure her that I was fine. I could see

Molly signal that she needed to get into the ladies, so I told her to go ahead.

"What do you want Rob," I sighed.

"I thought I would hear from you," Rob said. "After you had a brick through your window, I thought you'd be in contact."

"What?" I exclaimed. "How do you know about that?"

"Oh, um, someone told me," backtracked Rob. "I can't remember who it was. One of our mutual friends I guess."

"What mutual friend?" I asked. "Most of my friends don't like you, so I can't see that they would be telling you stuff about me".

"Thanks a bunch, Lily. Nice of you to kick a man while he's down," mumbled Rob. "Nothing changes does it?"

"What do you mean by that?" I asked.

"Forget it," said Rob. "I didn't come here to pick a fight".

"So why did you come here?" I asked.

"Because I wanted to see you," replied Rob. "I thought you might have come to your senses by now and realised that your rightful place is by my side. I want you back Lily. I was hoping that you would feel the same. I love you Lily, I always have. And I miss you."

I could feel my heart starting to race. I literally felt like a pressure cooker. I could feel the anger building up more and more. I held onto the door frame and stared at Rob.

"Well you are wrong," I stated. "I have no desire to see you whatsoever Rob. I've been much happier since we have been apart. Now please, buggar off and leave me alone. And for the record, I'm not here on my own. I'm here with my boyfriend. And also, you don't love me. If you did, you had a very funny way of showing it when we were together. I don't think you are capable of loving anyone other than yourself."

With that, I turned on my heel and stormed into the bathroom. My goodness, that man makes my blood boil. I can't believe he seriously thought that I might want to get back with him. And what about the brick through the window? Does that mean that it was him after all? If so, why did it take him until now to mention it? Or was he actually telling the truth for once, and he had heard about it rather than been directly involved himself?

As the questions started running through my head, Molly came out of the cubicle and washed her hands.

"Are you alright Lily?" she asked. "I'm sorry I left you with Rob, but I desperately needed the bathroom."

"It's no issue," I replied. "I've just told him where to go."

I filled Molly in on the conversation and she too wondered if Rob had thrown the brick through the window. The police had thought that it was kids, but maybe it was Rob after all. I was probably never going to know for sure, and I just wanted the whole thing forgotten. I'd moved on from Rob and I hoped that he would have too. He clearly hadn't yet, but after our latest conversation, hopefully he would now.

We headed back outside and rejoined our group. As I was filling Jack in on what had happened, Rob suddenly came barging over again. He bashed into Jack, presumably deliberately and pretended that he was sorry.

"Watch what you are doing mate," exclaimed Jack.

"You are no mate of mine," slurred Rob. "But you are welcome to Lily. She's a slut anyway."

Oh my goodness, I felt absolutely mortified. I hoped that Jack realised he was just being vindictive.

"Oh, right. You must be Rob," said Jack. "Get lost mate, before I call security."

At that the two security guys on the door headed over and took a firm hold of Rob before escorting him off of the premises.

"Are you ok Lily?" asked Jack. "I hope that didn't shake you up too much?"

"I'm fine," I reassured him. "He's such a knob. I can't believe that I was ever with him."

"Ah, don't worry about that," said Jack. "People change. I'm sure he was plenty charming enough when you were with him."

"Well, he was in the beginning. But he definitely has anger issues, especially after a drink or two. He's really not a nice man at all. I'm so glad that he's not a part of my life anymore. Seeing him now makes me realise how lucky I really am," I muse.

Jack gave me a hug, then headed off to the gents and I brought Georgia, Evie and Molly up to speed. They hadn't seen what had happened, although they caught the tail end of it and saw Rob being marched out of the bar by the security guards. Good riddance to bad rubbish was the general consensus.

Molly then headed off to the bar to buy the next round of drinks so Georgia, Evie & I headed to the dance floor for a bit of a boogy. They were playing some good dance anthems, so we spent twenty minutes enjoying ourselves. It took me back to my younger days when I was at University. The days of 'big fish, little fish, cardboard box".

After dancing to a few banging tunes we needed a rest and some drinks. We headed back to Molly and Jack. Molly handed us another drink each which we gratefully sipped on. The prosecco cocktail was tasty, yet refreshing.

"Where's Harry?" I asked Molly.

"I'm not sure," she replied. "I've not seen him since before I went to the bar."

We all scanned the bar, but couldn't see him. I walked towards the door, heading towards the security guards, when I suddenly spotted him. He was outside the window, chatting to somebody else. I couldn't see who it was but it was another guy and it looked like they were very deep in conversation. I went up to Molly and told her that I had seen Harry outside.

A few minutes later Harry came back into the bar. He went up to Molly and whispered in her ear. She glanced at me and whispered furiously back. I beckoned her over, and she came to me as Harry headed back outside.

"Is everything alright?" I asked. "What's going on?"

"Oh, it's fine," replied Molly. "Did you see who Harry was talking to outside?"

"No, they had their back to me so I couldn't see. Who was it?"

"It was James," she replied. She looked me straight in the eye. "Did you know he was coming?"

"Of course not," I said, shocked that she had asked me that. "Why would I know what he was doing?"

"I thought he might have contacted you in the last few days," she explained.

"No, I've not heard from him, and I wouldn't expect to to be honest," I replied.

Molly then took me to the side and explained that James and Jasmine had split up this week. She wanted to tell me, but didn't think my birthday was the appropriate time, especially as Jack had been with me much of the day. James had finished with Jasmine. Apparently he told her that he wanted them to just be friends.

"How do you feel?" she asked.

"I'm not sure really. A little surprised I guess," I stated.

At that, Harry came back in with James in tow. Molly and I rejoined the group, and I stood next to Jack. I took his hand to reassure him that everything was ok. He of course wasn't to know that I had no idea that James was going to turn up. James already knew everyone, so no introductions were required. But it did feel a little awkward all of a sudden.

A short time later, Jack headed off to the bar and James came up to talk to me.

"Happy Birthday Lily," he said. "Have you had a good day?"

"It's been amazing thank you. Are you ok?" I asked.

James looked me square in the eye, holding my eye contact for longer than was necessary.

"I will be in due course," he nodded.

166

He then proceeded to ask me if I had heard that he and Jasmine had split up. I told him that Molly had literally told me two minutes ago, and he looked a little disappointed.

"It was never the same, Lily. The Jasmine that returned was a very different Jasmine to the one that left. And I guess I changed too. I felt like I owed it to Jasmine to give our relationship a chance because of our history, but in hindsight, that was the wrong thing to do. I was happy with you. I was enjoying getting to know you. I was starting to fall in love with you. And all I've thought about in the last few weeks is you, and the fact is that whenever I've been with Jasmine I've been thinking about you."

I was stunned and rather taken aback. What a night this was turning out to be. I didn't really know what to say or do, and I was feeling very awkward about where this conversation was heading.

"Oh," I stuttered. "I don't really know what to say. Other than I'm sorry it didn't work out for you both. How has Jasmine taken it?"

"I don't expect you to say anything, Lily. It is what it is. I can't turn back the clock unfortunately, so I will just have to live with the consequences. I don't expect anything from you so don't worry. I'm aware I've more than likely missed the boat with you. And Jasmine is accepting of my decision. She must have realised that it wasn't working too, so I don't think it was a surprise."

Jack then returned with drinks for us all. I was so pleased he was back to rescue me from this conversation. I gratefully accepted my drink, tucked myself against his body, and enjoyed the feeling of his arm around me. It felt slightly weird in front of James, but it made me happy to feel like I was in the secure embrace of Jack's arms. I sipped at my drink and suddenly felt an overwhelming feeling of tiredness. I looked at my watch, seeing that it had gone 1 a.m. and suddenly thought longingly of my bed. I yawned, and Jack noticed.

"It's time we got you home, Princess. You look shattered," he suggested.

"Yes please," I replied. "I hadn't realised how truly tired I was."

"Don't leave on my account Jack, Lily," said James. "I was planning on heading off shortly anyway. I was just dropping in to catch up with Harry and say Happy Birthday to you Lily."

"It's no issue," replied Jack. "I think Lily is exhausted in any case. It's been a long day. Great fun, but tiring too."

I arranged to meet up with Molly for breakfast in the morning. We would need a good debrief after the rather hectic events of tonight. We then bid farewell to everyone. Jack took my hand and gently led me out of the bar. There were no taxi's waiting so we decided to walk home. It was only about twenty-five minutes' walk and we were both hot and sweaty from the bar, so it would give us time to cool down before bed.

Thirty minutes later we crawled into my bed. I was absolutely beat, and any thoughts of sex or chat went swiftly out of the window. I needed sleep. I snuggled up to Jack and as my head hit the pillow I do believe I was fast asleep just a few seconds later despite all the thoughts whirring around in my head.

Chapter 30

The next morning I woke up feeling pretty good. I hadn't drunk that much in the end, and it had been spread over a good number of hours. Plus a good dance always helps burn off the alcohol. It was lovely waking up with Jack this morning and I was hopeful that we would manage to make up for not having any action last night.

"Morning sexy," I whispered to Jack. "How are you feeling this morning?"

"Hmmmm," groaned Jack. "Very horny actually. I hope you are too?"

"Now that you mention it," I countered. "I could definitely do with a little birthday action."

"As you wish m'lady," granted Jack.

At that he turned onto his side and started to kiss me. He started at my lips, and gently pushed his tongue into my mouth. His kisses travelled down my neck onto my collarbone and then continued down to my breasts. He took one nipple into my mouth and his other hand crept downwards.

I was already very moist, so Jack was very able to slip a single finger inside me and spread the moisture around. He made sure that he was gently caressing my clitoris with one finger while sliding another finger inside me.

"You are so warm & wet," he muttered. "I could play with you forever."

"Well, I think it's time that I returned the favour a little bit," I replied.

I pushed at Jack's chest until he was lying on his back and I straddled him. I then peppered kisses from his lips, around to his ear, then down his neck. I left a trail of kisses all the way down his chest and stomach and down to his waist. I took his cock in my hand, it was already hard. I was very happy that he was well endowed – he was large, but not too massive. And I was quite slight in build and very tight in the downstairs area, so I wasn't sure I would be able to accommodate anything too massive.

I moved my hand down to between my own legs, and wiped a little of the moisture onto my hands. I then added a little spit and started to run my hand up and down Jack's cock. He quickly produced some pre-cum which added to the moisture. I could tell that he was enjoying the attention so I dipped my head and took the tip of his cock into my mouth.

He tasted good. Giving a blow job was not something that I gave out freely, and I definitely would only do it when I wanted to. To me I find that a blow job is quite an intimate experience, so I would never do this under any kind of duress.

I ran my lips down the length of his shaft, while using my hand to cup his balls and caress him at the same time. He seemed to like a combination of my lips, my tongue and my hand. I was careful to keep my teeth out of the way as I can't imagine that is a pleasant experience for any man. I could feel one of Jack's hands on the back of my head, but he wasn't putting any pressure on me. It was more of a caressing hand than anything else, and I liked it because I was able to gauge how much Jack enjoyed what I was doing to him.

After a couple more minutes of attention for Jack, I could tell that he was close to orgasm. Which he confirmed as he said,

170

"You have to stop, otherwise I'm going to cum in your mouth. And I don't want to do that. I want to feel myself inside of you."

I slid back up his body, whilst continuing to caress his cock with my hand. I joined my lips with his and enjoyed a deep kiss. Jack took hold of me and flipped us around so that he was on top of me. He reached over the side of the bed and pulled a condom out of his trouser pocket. Once he had put that on, he slowly entered me, not even needing to use any hands as he was so hard and I was so wet and turned on. Once he was fully inside me, he took each of my legs, one at a time, and hooked them over his shoulder. He then felt so deep inside me it felt absolutely sensational.

"Stay slow please Jack," I whispered. "You are so deep inside me that it will hurt if you go too hard right now."

"I fully intend to savour this moment Lily. I don't want to cum yet. I want this to last for a while," he whispered.

The feeling was absolutely sensational. I felt such a strong emotional connection to Jack, as well as an incredibly strong physical connection. I felt like telling him that I loved him, but I didn't want to do that in the heat of the moment, buoyed up by passion.

Despite our rhythm staying slow, I could feel the excitement building in both of us. We were getting close to orgasm even whilst trying not to. This build-up of tension is amazing. I truly love that feeling and the feeling of closeness that it brings. The first few weeks of sex with someone new is amazing. Finding out what each other likes, and enjoying the bond that develops between you.

"Lily," whispered Jack. "Can you turn around so that I can enter you from behind?"

"Do you mean doggy style, or back door action?" I asked.

"I meant doggy style," laughed Jack. "Although I'm quite glad that back door action might be available in the future."

"Well, we'll see about that in due course," I replied. "I've not actually ever tried that before. "

With that Jack pulled out from inside me, and I turned around. I could feel him aim his cock with his hands until he was back inside me. It was an interesting sensation, and very different from being able to look into his eyes. I shut my eyes, which helped to heighten the feeling of his touch and how deep inside of me that his cock felt. I could then feel Jack lean against my back and his hands went around me to caress my breasts. They felt pretty good and full with a little help from gravity, and he certainly seemed to appreciate them. He then snaked one arm around me and started to gently rub my clitoris whilst continuing to push his cock inside me.

Well that was pretty much it for me. I could feel the excitement building up towards explosion point. He obviously felt the same because I could feel his rhythm increase and he was pushing very deep inside me, but now it felt great. My body had accommodated him and I was loving the feeling.

"Harder Jack, I'm so close to orgasm," I commanded.

With that Jack grunted and I could feel the thrusts get harder. I could feel him pound into me and I loved it.

His fingers were still stroking my clitoris and he just seemed to have the perfect action as the combination of his hard cock thrusting and his fingers gently playing sent me higher and higher.

I felt myself tip over the edge as I squeezed with my internal muscles and I could feel the waves of orgasm from Jack inside me. We climaxed together and I felt fulfilled, hot and very sweaty. I immediately pushed his hand away as once I've had my orgasm my clitoris is so sensitive I can't cope with any more touching. I slowly sank onto the bed and I felt Jack collapse onto his elbows above me. He then gradually eased himself out of me, took care of the condom and lay on his side next to me.

I looked into his eyes and they were sparkling with satisfaction. It felt like we had this aura of passion surrounding us. I felt so happy, so content, and so sleepy. I didn't even feel like there was any need for us to talk.

I cuddled up into Jack's arms, rested my head on his chest, and listened to his heart rate and breathing rate slowly reduce, mirroring exactly what mine were doing. Just a few minutes later I could tell that Jack had dropped off to sleep, and I joined him shortly after.

An hour later Jack had headed home, and I was walking to the café to meet Molly. My head was spinning a little after the events of last night. When I arrived, Molly was already seated with a coffee so I ordered my tea & breakfast and we got the chat started.

"So, that was a pretty dramatic evening. We didn't get a chance to talk about it properly at the time," remarked Molly.

"Well, it was certainly eventful. I had not one, not two but three declarations of love on the same night. That's just insane," I spluttered having tried to start talking at the same time as taking a sip of tea.

"Wow," replied Molly. "I knew that James was still into you, but I didn't know anything about Rob. Honestly Lily, you are lucky. For you, men seem to be like buses. They don't come one at a time but they come in three's..."

"I wish they didn't though," I countered. "It just makes me feel awkward. Well, I feel awkward about James as I did like him a lot. I wouldn't go as far as to say that I was in love with him, but with time I think that could have been where we had ended up. But Rob. He doesn't love me. In fact, he doesn't love anyone but himself. He just misses controlling me, not loving me. He's a tosser. And I'm so glad that he's out of my life now".

"And what about Jack?" Molly asked.

"Well Jack is great. I am definitely falling for Jack, although I think it's too early to say I love him just yet. But, he certainly ticks all of my boxes and I genuinely enjoy spending time with him. And the nicest thing is that he likes me for me. He's not controlling. He doesn't get ridiculously jealous, but then I know he would have my back. He's fun, he's ambitious, he has a good work ethic. He has empathy and kindness. And he's sexy as anything. And I like the fact that he's well balanced in that he doesn't have vastly different moods and he seems in a good place in life."

"And you've talked about moving in, so you have definitely discussed a future together," added Molly.

"Yep, we have," I confirmed. "We both have similar wants and desires, and we've even talked about

174

having kids in due course. Not just yet of course, but maybe in a couple of years."

At that our breakfasts arrived. We carried out chatting and then I asked how things were going with Harry.

"They are good," said Molly. "We get on great, and we have fun together. The physical side of things is good and he seems in a good place too. We've talked about the future, but have decided we'd like to spend a little more time dating before moving in together, but we have similar wants & desires for the future. Harry is enjoying living with James at the moment, and he doesn't want to move out, plus I'm happy with how things are for the moment. Of course, that may change in time, but right now we are both content with where things are and how things are going."

"I'm so pleased for you. It's really nice that we both have found truly nice guys at the same time," I responded.

Later that morning as I was walking home after finishing breakfast, I couldn't help but smile to myself. And then I actually burst out laughing. I couldn't get the 'Men Are Like Buses' comment that Molly made to me out of my head. I'm sure this old guy shuffling along the pavement towards me thought that I was absolutely bonkers. He must have thought that I was talking to myself like some mad woman.

Who knows what the future will bring. But I don't need any more buses. I'm quite happy riding the bus that I'm already on all the way to the depot.

Printed in Great Britain
by Amazon

38324810R00101